THE CRUISE
OF A
DEATHTIME

The Cruise of a Deathtime

Marian Babson

Walker and Company
New York

c. 1

First published in the United States of America
in 1984 by the Walker Publishing Company, Inc.

Published simultaneously in Canada by John Wiley & Sons
Canada, Limited, Rexdale, Ontario.

Library of Congress Cataloging in Publication Data

Babson, Marian.
   The cruise of a deathtime.

   I. Title.
PS3552.A25C7 1984   813'.54   83-40415
ISBN 0-8027-5588-7

Printed in the United States of America

10 9 8 7 6 5 4 3 2 1

PROLOGUE

The *Empress Josephine*, two days out from Miami on a non-stop voyage to her registered home port of Nhumbala, carried five hundred and twenty-three passengers and two hundred and fifty crew. Her main cargo hold was filled with crates labelled 'Dried Milk' and 'Medical Supplies', all marked with the outline of a wine glass, the international symbol for 'Fragile — Handle with Care'.

Another part of the hold contained a motley collection of passengers' vehicles, ranging from Cadillacs to Dormobiles to motor-cycles.

In still another part of the hold was the cargo that no one mentioned: a supply of coffins, some of which might be needed during the long voyage.

By the very nature of things, the people who could afford both the time and the money to take an extended cruise tended to be elderly, retired, perhaps in poor health. Nevertheless, the spirit of adventure still burned in their hearts. They looked forward to exploring strange shores and making new friends; those still active in the business world hoped for new contacts and large export orders at the end of the voyage.

Others hoped for romance — even with a small 'r'. Some looked to the restorative powers of a ten-day sea voyage to recover their health. Some frankly expected to be bored at least part of the time.

All of them planned on long lazy days in deckchairs, plenty of duty-free drinks, good food, lavish entertainment, fun and surprises — as promised by the colourful brochure advertising the cruise.

None of them planned on being buried at sea . . .

CHAPTER 1

No one really expected the Captain to appear for dinner on the first couple of nights out, so they were not disappointed by the empty chair at the head of the table. It was enough that they were at the Captain's table themselves, favoured above all others. They eyed each other covertly over their menus, wondering at the degree of fortune or celebrity that had led to the others being thus honoured.

Two of their number were instantly recognizable: The Ordways (or Odd-ways, as the irrepressible Quizmaster used to put it, while the studio audience shrieked with laughter); Mortie and Hallie, the couple whose agonies and triumphs the nation had followed breathlessly through eleven weeks of increasingly difficult-to-impossible questions on the Coast-to-Coast television quiz show *The Loot of a Lifetime*. Each week had piled up the loot, consumer durables to stoke dreams of avarice; each week brought the agonizing decision whether to retire quietly with their loot, or to return next week to stake it all on their ability to answer the unknown questions in the Quizmaster's Little Black Book. Their presence here was proof that they had triumphed, winning not only the Loot of a Lifetime, but climaxing it by winning the Cruise of a Lifetime, as well.

They sat side by side, glittering with the diamonds that formed part of the loot, cheerfully acknowledging the tentative smiles of passengers nodding to them from adjoining tables, the king and queen of the audience-participation quiz shows. Their shipmates preened in the reflected glory; the presence of the Ordways set the seal on everything they had been promised in the travel brochure. They were, indeed, on the Cruise of a Lifetime.

Mrs Anson-Pryce was not so sure. She had expected a better class of person at the Captain's table. Not that she hadn't watched that quiz show and been just as amused as anyone else by the . . . the *antics* . . . of the pair, particularly the wife, whenever they had answered a question correctly. However, watching cavorting eccentrics on a small screen was quite different from sharing a table with them. One could only hope that the . . . the female creature . . . wouldn't go into one of her famous back somersaults if her . . . mate . . . managed to negotiate the waiter's question, 'What would you like, sir?' successfully.

The waiter was hovering over her now, she looked up briefly and encountered watching eyes from across the table. She gave a tight-lipped smile and ordered swiftly. Relinquishing her menu, she lowered her gaze to her wrist and toyed abstractly with her diamond bracelet, refusing the risk of further eye contact with anyone at the table.

Herr Otto von Schreiber and his dumpy Frau were on the other side of the empty chair. No matter that the Frau's diamonds were bigger and brighter than her own, they were another couple one must be hesitant about acknowledging socially. It was not just their porcine appearance; their age was also against them. One could never quite look at a German male in that age range without the silent question forming at the back of one's mind: 'And what did *you* do in the Great War, Daddy?'

The final couple at the table were so inoffensive as to be nondescript. They obviously had money enough or they wouldn't be on board, but one rather doubted that they would have an entry in the Social Register.

It was really *too* bad. The Captain was going to be the only person at the table worth speaking to — and everyone knew that Captains were unreliable table companions. They tended to avoid communal meals at every opportunity, pleading such feeble excuses as fog, storm, or unspecified urgent business which required their presence on the Bridge. And so they neglected the passengers — the guests — at their table. No sense of responsibility at all!

A raucous laugh erupted from the table immediately behind her and Mrs Anson-Pryce repressed a shudder. *Parvenus* to a man — and a woman. Especially the drunkard — she knew the signs — who appeared to be sitting back-to-back with her.

It was too late to change her seat now. Even if the dumpy little Hausfrau were willing to switch places with her, it was quite certain that the Herr would not allow it, suspecting some obscure lowering of status. And if she were to exchange with the drab little Lawton woman, it would not only take her away from the Captain, it would place her next to that obnoxious Mortimer Ordway.

She repressed another shudder. She was trapped.

Carl Daniels, the Purser, leaned attentively towards the lady on his left. No one observing him would have guessed that his thoughts were elsewhere. He smiled automatically, making the right responses, while his gaze swept across the dining salon checking for errors of omission and commission, possible future trouble spots — or trouble-makers — anything that was not quite right, which might disturb the passengers or lessen their comfort. Although he disdained the usage on some modern ships where the Purser was called the Hotel Manager, that was essentially what he was. He prided himself that he was a good one.

Right now, he was an extremely annoyed one. His Assistant Purser had missed the ship. Waring had never let him down like that before. Indeed, on any other sailing this season it would not have mattered. On the usual island-hopping week-long cruise, any crew member who missed his sailing could take a plane to the next port of call and catch up with the *Empress Josephine* there.

This trip, however, was scheduled straight through to Nhumbala. Ten days without touching port. After they had off-loaded the cargo of urgent medical supplies and the few passengers — most of them businessmen — who were leaving the ship there, the *Empress Josephine* would make her way slowly back to Miami, stopping at some of the beauty-spot islands along the way.

That meant he'd be short-handed until Waring caught up with the ship at Nhumbala — *if* Waring bothered to. He might not think it worth his while and just wait in Florida for the next sailing. Or he might already have signed on with some other ship; he'd been showing signs of restlessness of late. True, he was supposed to give proper notice, but it was not unknown for sailors to jump ship when they felt like it. He had thought better of Waring, but he had been wrong before.

Not often. Expertly he assessed the passengers at the tables within his view. The usual mixture: some who would just want to lie back in deckchairs and bask in the sun; others who would discover that a sea cruise wasn't quite what they had expected and chafe at the restrictions of shipboard life.

The woman sitting beside Captain Falcon's empty chair, now, was a complainer. Captain Falcon *would* be pleased. The heavy-set German woman on his other side would not cheer him either. There would be a good many formal meals skipped on this crossing.

There was a familiar figure at the table beyond. Not the face: the type. A drunk. There was one — if not more — on almost every cruise. They'd have to keep an eye on his intake and monitor his whereabouts. Not, unfortunately, for fear that he might fall overboard — no such luck, the God who most unfairly reserved his attention for fools, drunks and madmen would see to that — but to make sure that he didn't constitute a nuisance to the other passengers.

As Carl Daniels swung his gaze around the dining salon, the individual faces blurred and melted into the familiar haze. Over the next few days, some would emerge sharply — for good or ill — and become memorable. Others would remain nondescript and nameless for the entire voyage, no reason to like or dislike them, nor to remember them. These were the majority of the passengers. The only problem would be if this were their second, third or fourth trip aboard the *Empress Josephine*. In that case, they would expect to be hailed with delight as Old Faithfuls.

No matter. A quick survey of the passenger list on the VDU would sort out the repeaters and suitable arrangements for special treatment could be made. Unfortunately, that was part of Waring's job. Waring, who had missed his sailing.

Bloody Waring . . .

D. D. Smithers was having a wonderful time. He usually had a wonderful time. If the party palled, a few more drinks took care of the situation. It was the secret of Life — the secret of everything. A secret he could see it would be necessary to impart to the people at his table.

They were the usual collection of dull bores. It was strange the way Fate always seemed to land him with Puritans, teetotallers and others of that ilk. The woman across from him had already sniffed disparagingly three times — and they were only halfway through the soup. The one beside him had recoiled and waved air to her nose when he had leaned over to speak to her.

Somewhere aboard this ship there must be more congenial company. Perhaps even congenial female company. He would have to seek it out.

Meanwhile . . . He brightened and poured more wine into his glass — the others were drinking water from the large cut-glass jug in the middle of the table — that just went to show what they were like. It would be a dreary voyage if he were stuck with them all the way across. Perhaps, when he found that more congenial company, he could change his table. There would be no objections from this lot if he did. They'd be glad to see the back of him. Well, it was their loss.

Meanwhile . . . he refreshed his glass. Charity set in. Maybe he ought to give them an idea of what they'd be missing.

'Did you ever hear —?' He leaned over to the dowager on the other side. 'Did you ever hear the one about the impotent Bishop and the chorus girl?'

Outside, the shore of another island slipped out of sight. The *Empress Josephine*, lit from stem to stern, was a bright jewel on the dark sea, observed enviously by people on the distant shore. It would take another thirty-six hours for her to thread her way through the islands and break free into open ocean.

After that, she would be on her own. A small floating city, beyond the reach of land-locked laws, under the sovereign rule of her Captain, administered by her officers, knowing no higher authority to protect her in case of trouble.

The *Empress Josephine* sailed serenely through the night.

CHAPTER 2

The stewardess closed the door gently, silently — as though it could make any difference — and hurried down the passage-way, hoping that she would not encounter any passengers. She could not trust herself to try to smile.

Carl Daniels saw her coming. The tightly-controlled haste, the frozen mask of her face, warned him. The first crisis of the cruise had arrived. It must be a serious one — Joan Fletcher did not get upset easily.

He nodded in response to her urgent signal as she walked past him to the rear of the Purser's Office. 'Come back in an hour and I'll see what we can do,' he said to the complaining passenger who wished to change her cabin.

'Sorry —' he smiled at the two others as he pulled down the metal latticework grille and locked it — 'we'll be open again in an hour.' Ignoring the grumbles, he walked to the back of the office where Joan was using the telephone.

'Urgent,' she said to the person at the other end of the line. 'A Deck, Cabin 223. I'll meet you there with the key. Although . . .' she hesitated, 'I'm afraid it's too late for you to be of any help. I'm afraid they've been . . . gone . . . for several hours.'

'They?' Daniels cursed silently. 'What's happened?'

'Married couple.' Joan hung up on the doctor and turned to face him. 'Looks like some sort of overdose.'

'Both of them?' He was incredulous. 'Were they drug addicts?'

'Hardly likely. I didn't stop to examine them, but I'd say they were the wrong age group. Dr Parker should be able to tell.'

'Right, you'd better get back to the cabin and let him in. I'll be along in a couple of minutes.' Daniels nodded approvingly as she moved off smoothly, without undue haste. He knew that, like himself, she wanted to run, but the sight of two of the ship's crew running full-tilt along the corridors would spread panic among the passengers, especially the first-time ones who were preternaturally aware that only a shell of metal lay between them and the briny deep.

He riffled unseeingly through a card file for the benefit of anyone who might be watching. (More acting was done by the crew than by the professional entertainers on some voyages.) When he judged enough time had elapsed since Joan's departure, he replaced the file, locked the office and sauntered casually in the direction she had taken. When he rounded the corner and found no passengers in sight, he lengthened his stride.

'Joan —' He tapped at the door of 223. It swung back noiselessly just far enough to let him slip into the cabin.

Dr Parker was bent over one of the recumbent forms. He glanced up briefly, shook his head and turned to the form in the other bed.

Carl Daniels leaned against the door and watched as Dr Parker pulled back the duvet and checked respiration and pulse. He did not allow himself to hope. Both bodies were too still, lifeless.

'Second day out,' he complained softly. 'This is one hell of a start to the cruise. What happened?'

'Suicide pact?' Dr Parker hazarded, still bent over the man's body.

'Why?' Daniels asked.

'Who knows?' Dr Parker straightened up and shrugged. 'Personal problems . . . ill health of one or both . . .' He picked up a small bottle from the nearest bedside table and squinted at the label. 'The usual sleeping pills . . . empty.' He grimaced and set it down again. 'One or both has trouble sleeping . . . had.'

'Why do it here? I mean,' Daniels said, 'why pay for an expensive luxury cruise and kill yourself the first night out? It would be easier to understand if they had a final fling and killed themselves on the last night out. Just before we reached shore and all their problems closed round them again. But . . . first night out?'

'Perhaps they couldn't stand the food.' Parker shrugged again. 'Felt they couldn't face it for the rest of the cruise and decided to cut their losses.'

'Brilliant diagnosis, Doctor.' Daniels had never been in sympathy with the graveyard humour of the medical profession. 'Are you going to write it up for the medical journals?'

'I've checked the medicine cabinet —' Joan came out of the bathroom carrying a collection of small bottles. 'One of them seems to have had heart trouble.'

'There you are. Perhaps one of them died and the other decided not to be left behind.' It made minimally more sense to Daniels, but was still not satisfactory.

'Without calling the doctor for help first?' Joan put her finger on the flaw. It was against human nature not to summon immediate help for a stricken partner, even though the situation seemed hopeless.

'It's a thought, anyway.' Daniels looked at the doctor. 'Perhaps you could examine the bodies. Do an autopsy.'

'I'm not a pathologist.' Dr Parker looked pained. 'Nor does this ship have facilities for that sort of thing. Furthermore, what are the next of kin going to say if we hand over the bodies all carved up?' He paused. 'Or do we just bury them at sea? I've never lost a patient . . at sea.'

'*Mal de mer* isn't usually fatal,' Daniels agreed. He had not missed the doctor's hesitation. Suddenly he wished he knew more about the man.

Jack Parker had signed on at the beginning of the season,

carrying out his medical duties efficiently and unremarkably from September to this present moment in mid-January. Not that there had been anything to test his skill. Seasickness and sunburn were the most common maladies, varied by the occasional grumbling appendix or tourist tummy picked up by an unwise menu choice on a shore excursion. He upheld the social end well enough at his table although he did not mix with the passengers nor, for that matter, with the crew. Whether by nature or circumstances, he seemed to be essentially a loner.

'What *do* we do, Carl?' Joan set the medicine bottles down on the dressing-table beside a small framed picture of a pair of toddlers — twins. If there were grandchildren, then there would be a son or daughter who would have to be notified.

'See if you can find their passports,' he directed. 'See who's listed as next of kin.'

'It can't be suicide —' Joan began searching. 'They haven't left any note.'

'Contrary to popular opinion,' Dr Parker said, 'only about fifteen per cent of people who commit suicide leave notes. That's why the suicide statistics aren't higher. The police give them the benefit of the doubt and list the death as accidental in order to spare the relatives.'

'I suppose it couldn't be an accidental overdose?' Joan suggested hopefully.

'Both of them?'

Joan met the sardonic gaze and flushed. Silently she returned to her task, reaching for the woman's handbag which was tucked in a corner beside the bed. The passport was in the inner zippered compartment.

'Her eyes were hazel,' she said irrelevantly and found herself fighting back tears. The small vanity, meticulously identifying her eye colour as *hazel*, rather than green or brown, brought the dead woman to life momentarily, like the thong sandal or gold necklace turned up on an archæological site which suddenly bridged the gap across centuries so that you could almost reach out and touch the original owner.

'Never mind that,' the doctor said impatiently. 'Who's the next of kin?'

'There's a son —' she held the passport out to Carl Daniels, opened at the page — 'in New Jersey.'

'Right.' Carl accepted it reluctantly; there was a very unpleasant task ahead of him. Ordinarily the problem would be referred to Head Office ashore, but they were a small company and the office worked overtime for several days before a sailing, then took a long weekend after the ship was safely out of port. This was Saturday and the office wouldn't open again until Wednesday. They couldn't help and the situation couldn't wait.

'I'll telephone the son,' Carl said, 'and see what arrangements the family will settle for, bearing in mind that we can't ruin our schedule by diverting to a local port to drop off the bodies.

'Meanwhile —' he tried to keep sarcasm out of his voice, there was no point in antagonising Parker — 'perhaps the doctor would be good enough to give the bodies as thorough an inspection as possible in the circumstances and let us know if he can come to some conclusion about what might have happened. The family will want to know.'

'Perhaps the Purser —' Dr Parker was equally polite and careful — 'would be good enough to ask a few questions of the family. 'I'd like to know whether either of them had a fatal illness — or believed they had. It would also be interesting to know their financial status — an impending bankruptcy could also explain the course they've chosen.'

'I'll try, but the family wouldn't be likely to tell me. Oh, they might admit there had been health worries, but I don't think they'd confide about money problems.'

'As a rule, people don't,' Parker agreed. 'They'd rather deny everything — especially suicide — and shift the blame on to us in some way.'

'A lawsuit we don't need.' They were in perfect accord now. 'So do the best sort of examination you can and see if you can find anything we can use to defend ourselves.'

'I'll try . . . but here?' Parker raised his eyebrows and looked around: At the beds, too low to stoop over comfortably for a prolonged examination; at the lighting, low-keyed to give the effect of opulence, but useless for exacting work.

'No,' Daniels said. 'We'll lock up the cabin for the time being. I'll have the bodies moved to your hospital during Boat Drill this afternoon. All the passengers will be on deck and out of the way then.'

Pesky Calhoun stood more or less at attention and tried to smother a yawn. He watched as the First Officer went down the line at Lifeboat No.5 for the third time, pausing to re-tie the straps of a life-jacket quite unnecessarily. The passenger was neither young nor pretty and the straps had been tied correctly in the first place.

Overhead, the loudspeaker crackled and coughed, then began spitting out the usual spiel again, this time in Spanish. They had already had it in French, Nhumbalan and German — despite the fact that the only Krauts on board were those two at the Captain's table and they spoke pretty good English. What next — Serbo-Croatian?

Eventually they might even run it in English and give all those long-suffering passengers standing around so patiently a break. In fact, they had usually got to English and dismissed everyone long before this. What was going on?

'Good afternoon, ladies and gentlemen, welcome aboard the *Empress Josephine* . . .' That was better, they were running Captain Falcon's tape now. The passengers would be free to disperse once his bit was over. They had already been standing around longer than usual.

Not that the passengers realized that. Every ship was different, with its own selection of languages according to the most frequently carried nationalities. Instructions varied somewhat, from ship to ship, as well.

'I would remind all passengers who smoke to be extremely careful about the disposal of their cigarettes.' That instruction was constant with every ship but — Pesky frowned — this was the second time Captain Falcon had repeated it. He listened more closely. They weren't using a tape, after all. The Captain was speaking in person, more slowly than on tape and with greater emphasis.

'Do not throw lighted cigarettes over the side of the ship. The ship is moving and the wind can carry them back on board where they might start a fire. I repeat, *never* throw your cigarette over the side —'

Fire at sea was one of the worst things that could happen in the nautical world, but surely the old boy was pushing it a bit. Or was there something he knew that the rest of them didn't? Had there been some sort of tip-off that they were carrying a suspected arsonist this voyage? Or perhaps one of the passengers had a notorious reputation for being careless with cigarettes.

Pesky looked around but everyone he could see looked as normal as anyone who took these cruises. After a while, they all began to look alike. This was his third season as Cruise Director on the *Empress Josephine* and he was beginning to think that it was time he looked for a job ashore again. Or perhaps a better ship.

Cosmo Carpenter caught his eye and winked at him from the next group along, mustered at Lifeboat Station No.3. Beside Cosmo, Connie sent him a little grimace of excitement. It was all right for them, this was their very first voyage as on-board entertainers. Wait until they found out how much work they were going to have to do. If this weren't such a cheapjack line, there'd be at least three other entertainers and a second band.

'I thank you, ladies and gentlemen, and I wish you a very happy voyage.' Captain Falcon finished and the groups at the Lifeboat Stations began to disperse, untangling their straps and freeing themselves of the cumbersome life-jackets as they went along.

'They're taking good care of us, I see.' One of the passengers looked down at his life-jacket approvingly. It had all the safety devices. One pocket contained a packet of bright orange aniline dye which would spread out and colour the water for daytime visibility; another pocket had a whistle; a small light bulb attached to a waterproof battery in another pocket provided for night-time visibility. If you went overboard from the *Empress Josephine* your chances of being found and rescued were very good indeed.

'Nothing but the best for our passengers.' Pesky beamed automatically. 'If you travel on this ship, you've got to be a survivor!'

It was just bad luck that the Purser walked by in time to catch the last remark. If looks could kill! *Done it again, Pesky. All four feet in the old mouth.* Maybe he'd be looking for that shore job sooner than he thought.

Oh well, so he'd never make the top of the Purser's Popularity Parade. At least they couldn't put him in a lifeboat with a few provisions and leave him adrift in open sea. There were laws about that sort of thing these days. Equity wouldn't like it, either.

Equity. He winced mentally, remembering his pride when he first got his Equity card. All those hopes and dreams and what had they come down to? Cruise Director on a third-rate liner bumbling around the Caribbean shuttling the punters from one tourist trap to another in weekly relays. Once a year they made this long voyage to Nhumbala carrying medical supplies and Famine Relief Aid; it was a condition of being allowed to sail under the Nhumbalan flag of convenience. Some convenience, the seamen said, when we've got to hit *that* port once a year. They didn't mind it all that much, though, and the *Empress Josephine* featured it as the Gala Cruise of the year. It seemed to pull enough passengers, the ship was three-quarters full.

The trouble was keeping them amused for ten solid days at sea. Shuffleboard, deck tennis and skeet-shooting were all right during the daytime, but in the evening bingo and horse-racing quickly palled. Some would always be happy with films, thank heaven, and they had taken on a dozen new feature films just before sailing. There was no percentage in that, however; the

Line preferred to have its human cargo spending money in the night club or gambling casino. They were better off doing that than dancing, even if the sea held smooth. Most of them didn't look up to more than a lap or two around the floor before a coronary set in.

He could see very clearly that he was going to have to think up a lot more sedentary entertainment on this cruise. And all he had to work with was a four-piece band and Cosmo and Connie Carpenter, Entertainers Extraordinaire. They'd better be *extraordinaire* — they were going to have to spread themselves pretty thin.

Of course, he brightened, there was that truncated version of *Design for Living* they had talked about. With a part for him. He could learn the lines easily enough and it would be a relief to do some good honest acting again, a genuine part instead of playing the fool offstage. The trouble was, they couldn't stretch it out for more than two matinees and one evening performance, and then everyone interested would have seen it and be looking to them to come up with something else to entertain them.

The deck was almost deserted now. Everyone had returned to their cabins to stow away their life-jackets before coming back on deck. Pesky recognized the couple now going inside as the Ordways.

Perhaps they'd be willing to do something to help out — not that he'd put it to them like that. But . . . they might be willing to compere a Quiz Show along the lines of the one that had made them so famous — and affluent. They might like to be on the other side of the fence, asking the questions for a change.

Yes, put it to them like that. Do it for a lark. What else could you offer them? Pesky recalled the final night of their triumphant success. The Quizmaster had pointed out that, if they were to switch on all the electrical appliances they had won at the same time, they could black out a small city.

They'd have to be willing to do it for laughs. What else could you offer a couple who had everything?

'So much for the financial theory,' Carl Daniels said. He should have known it was unlikely. People who were travelling on this ship weren't short of money. 'The son is chartering a cabin cruiser to rendezvous with us and collect the bodies. He wants Mom and Dad to be given a decent burial in the old family plot.'

'You can't blame him for that.' Dr Parker was more in sympathy with the landlubbers than the sailors. It was no tradition among the passengers to be buried at sea. 'Just lucky for him that it happened while we were still close enough to shore for it to be possible. Lucky for us, too. Can't say I like the idea of carrying a couple of sealed coffins around till we got back to Miami.'

'It wouldn't have been that long,' Daniels countered absently. 'We'd have put them ashore at Nhumbala and contacted a local undertaker to handle the red tape and transfer them to the airport to fly them back.' He sighed. 'The son sounded half out of his mind. Says it can't be suicide, it must be something wrong aboard ship. They were perfectly healthy and happy when they sailed. He's determined to blame it on us.'

'Just as well I didn't do any cutting.' Dr Parker poured drinks. 'That would really have made them suspicious. They'd think we were trying to hide something. By the way, I'm pretty sure it was the sleeping pills. I don't see how that can be blamed on the Line.'

'If there's a way, they'll find it.' Daniels lapsed into gloomy silence.

'How do we manage?' Dr Parker prodded. 'Without upsetting the other passengers, I mean? I've had a couple of close calls, but this is the first time I've actually had anyone die on board ship. What's the drill?'

'We'll bring up two coffins from the hold.' Daniels stirred uneasily. He should be seeing to it now, but was curiously reluctant to leave the doctor's quarters. It wasn't that he liked the man very much, it must be the task he was shirking.

'During dinner, while the passengers are all out of the way.' Jack Parker was learning fast.

'That's right. By then the skipper of the chartered cruiser will
have contacted me about the rendezvous. He'll cooperate.' Men
of the sea stuck together at times like this. 'We'll arrange it for
the early hours of the morning — he couldn't get here much
earlier than three or four a.m., anyway. We'll offload the coffins
and the cruiser will be out of sight over the horizon before any of
the passengers are awake.'

'No problem, then.' Parker topped up their glasses.

'No.' Daniels stared down into the amber depths. 'Not for us.
But it's not very pleasant for the next of kin. An autopsy won't
tell the son what was going on in their minds. The family may
never know why they did such a thing.'

Both of them? The anguished, incredulous cry of their son
would remain in his memory for a long time. It was not
surprising that, in the first wave of shock and grief, the man
would try to blame it on some negligence aboard ship, some
grievous fault on the part of the shipping line. A man did not
expect when he said a happy, cheerful goodbye to parents off on
a holiday cruise to have them returned to him in a pair of
wooden coffins. No wonder he was trying to make some sense of
the nightmare. How could he face the fact that he was not
enough to comfort them, that they had chosen to go away and
leave him?

Daniels shook his head and gulped at the whisky. He knew
that he would be haunted by that anguished cry, which echoed
his own doubts:

'*Both* of them?'

CHAPTER 3

'This ship was disgracefully noisy all through the night!' Mrs
Anson-Pryce was an old hand at cruising. She knew what was
right and proper aboard ship and the *Empress Josephine* was
falling short of the ideal by a wide margin.

'Surely you must have noticed it?' She looked around the luncheon table for agreement. 'It was quite insupportable. That was why I missed breakfast. By the time I got to sleep, I was so exhausted I slept straight through. You must have heard it?'

'We were pretty tired ourselves.' Mary Lawton answered for herself and her husband. 'We fell asleep as soon as our heads hit the pillow.'

'That's right. Us, too.' Mortimer Ordway beamed across at the Lawtons. 'The ship could have sunk last night and we wouldn't even have noticed. Not until we had to start swimming.' His wife giggled and nodded.

'Well, it was quite dreadful!' Mrs Anson-Pryce stuck to her guns. 'I trust it won't be like that again tonight, or I — I shall —'

'What will you do, sweetheart?' D. D. Smithers leaned back in his chair, bumping back to back with her chair, and twisted round to leer at her. 'Get out and walk?'

He was drunk again already. Or possibly still drunk from the night before. She pretended she had not heard him, refusing to dignify his intrusion by an answer.

'Surely, Herr von Schreiber —' she turned to the glowering German — '*you* must have heard all the noise?'

'No.' He looked at her with disapproval, perhaps dislike. 'Ve did not hear a thing. This is an excellent ship. Vell run. There was no disturbance in the night.'

'I can assure you, there was.' She glanced at the empty chair beside her with dissatisfaction. 'However, it appears that I am the only person at this table aware of it. I shall complain to the Captain personally — if he ever deigns to join us. And if the situation does not improve —' she raised her voice to drown out the faint but unmistakable Bronx cheer coming from behind her — 'I shall write a letter of complaint to the Chairman of the Shipping Line!'

The brochure distinctly said that there were six bars on the ship. In clear black and white: 'The *Empress Josephine* has six delightful bars for the delectation of passengers. From the formal splendour of the Versailles Night Club to the intimacy of the Bonaparte Bistro Bar, our staff are there to serve you delicious cocktails and rum punches, always attentive to your every desire. Try the *Coronation de Joséphine* and other specialities of the ship and they will make you feel like royalty yourself.'

Plain as could be — well, almost. Even allowing for the excesses of Tourist-Speak and Fractured Franglais, the message was clear and distinct: there were six bars on board.

So far, D. D. Smithers had found only three of them. There were three more to be discovered. It was a challenge, the sort he liked best. The sort he could really rise to.

Let others climb Everest or sail solo across the Atlantic — there was no accounting for taste. To each, his own ambition. It was the proud boast of D. D. Smithers that there had never been a bar, pub or saloon within a radius of twenty miles of him that he hadn't been able to find and enter, no unknown drink that he had not sampled.

The ship lurched gently and D.D. lurched with it, caroming lightly from one wall of the narrow corridor to the other. He was exploring — bar-hunting, if you like — and the motion of the ship was more noticeable in these lower decks. Perhaps too noticeable. Perhaps they wouldn't site a bar this low just because of that. If people felt too much motion, it might put them off their booze, make them think they'd had too much to drink already. That would never do.

Try the next deck up, that ought to be more promising. D.D. reached the end of the corridor and emerged into a small circular lobby. There were stairs on either side and, more important, a lift. He rolled across the lobby and began pushing buttons indiscriminately. He'd never seen this lift before, perhaps it would lead to one of the hidden bars.

He waited hopefully, swaying companionably in rhythm with the ship. Or perhaps it was just him swaying. Didn't matter. Everybody rolled a bit and swayed a bit on a ship. No one ever noticed.

The lift seemed a long time coming. Perhaps someone was holding it on one of the upper decks, or perhaps it was out of order. Might only have an operator at certain times of the day and this wasn't one of them. No lights had gone on to indicate that his call had been accepted, no promising humming sound was coming from behind the closed doors.

Abandon hope — abandon ship. No luck here. Which way now — up or down?

Upward, ever upward. D.D. grasped the handrail firmly and began to pull himself up the stairs. It definitely was the ship. The stairs seemed to be trying to roll away from him with a skittish playfulness, leaving him momentarily suspended and weightless before gravity reasserted itself and slammed his foot down on the next stair with more force than he had intended. The party was getting rough. Needed another little drink to settle it down.

There! Head of the stairs and didn't stumble once. Who said he couldn't do it? He was in another small circular lobby, but there was a wider and altogether more promising-looking corridor leading aft from it.

Furthermore, one of the ship's officers was moving purposefully down that corridor. D.D. recognised that walk — it was that of a man heading for a drink, if ever he'd seen one. Hopefully, he followed along. Perhaps he'd be led to one of those three elusive bars.

Halfway down the passageway, the officer disappeared. D.D. hurried to the door he had gone through and opened it, then stopped short in disappointment.

It led into a narrow uncarpeted corridor fitfully lit by dim unshaded overhead lights. The officer was nowhere in sight. Directly facing the door was the notice: NO ADMITTANCE. CREW ONLY.

Well, if they felt like that about it . . . D.D. backed away and closed the door. He didn't want to go behind the scenes of the *Empress Josephine*, anyway. Yet he found the restriction irksome. At the prices they charged, the passengers ought to be allowed into the crow's-nest, if they wanted to go up there.

The best way to investigate the crew's quarters was to make friends with one of the crew. He had already missed his chance with that officer, he should have caught up with him, walked along beside him and then, probably, he'd have been invited below. Because that had been a man heading for a good stiff drink if D.D. had ever seen one and, in his life, he had seen many.

Of course. There would be a bar for the crew. A separate bar in their own quarters, where they could get an honest drink, unlike those served to the passengers. A drink a man didn't have to fight his way through the fruit salad to taste.

In that case, there were seven bars on board. D.D.'s eyes gleamed. Even after he had found the remaining three, there would still be a challenge.

But, play the game. First, he had to notch up the advertised bars before he looked for the other. Fair was fair, first you checked out the bars they told you about before you went for the one they tried to keep secret.

Happily D.D. nodded as the ship lurched as though in agreement. Then, weaving slowly, he made his way down the corridor to continue his quest.

'And-one-and-two . . . and-three-and-four . . . Just a little high-er, Mrs Lawton. You can do it, I know you can.' Connie Carpenter's bright smile did not fade as she put her Keep-Fit Class through its faltering paces.

'Then you . . . know more . . . than I do,' Mary Lawton gasped. Her knee rose another half inch and balked.

'That's better . . .' Connie made a mental bet with herself that her class would be halved by tomorrow afternoon's meeting. Especially if the ship continued rolling. Stretching out in the deckchairs was going to seem a lot more enticing to the pupils.

For that matter, she'd rather be stretched out in a deckchair herself. It was only the third day out, but she was beginning to realize just what they had let themselves in for. Their show in the Versailles Night Club had lasted until one a.m., then they had mingled with the passengers and had a few drinks, forgetting the hour Cosmo had to rise in order to pace the early morning joggers around the Promenade Deck.

Immediately after breakfast, there had been the Deck Games, the opening jousts in a Shuffleboard and Deck Tennis Tournament which would go on until the last day out. After morning bouillon had been served, those in search of learning had gathered in the Library for what would be their daily sortie into Conversational Nhumbalan. ('Good morning.' 'How much is that ivory carving?' 'Too much. Have you anything cheaper?' 'Yes, if you will deliver it to the ship.' 'Do you accept travellers cheques?') Taught by, guess who? Your own, your very own, Connie Carpenter — who was only one sentence ahead of the class herself.

Then lunch, followed by a matinee performance of a one-act play, followed by late-afternoon Keep-Fit Class.

Not that Cosmo was having it any easier. From overhead came the sporadic sound of shots where Cosmo was releasing his traps for the clay pigeon shooting on the Sports Deck. There had been complaints yesterday that he was not fast enough and it didn't sound as though he had speeded up any. It was not his favourite task of the day. Any noise louder than applause hurt his ears.

'Like this, Mary —' Obviously Hallie Ordway was pining for the spotlight. Connie recognized the symptoms. Hallie pranced out of the line-up of well-fleshed, slightly puffing women and flipped across the dance floor in a series of cartwheels.

Not even Connie could do that. Hallie Ordway *had* to be double-jointed or something.

There were gasps of admiration — and envy — and a generous splatter of applause. Connie froze a bright smile on her face and joined in the applause, trying not to resent the fact that Hallie had just stolen her show. *She* was supposed to be the one whose suppleness was a goal to be achieved.

'Do the back-flip, Hallie,' a voice begged. 'Like you did on television when you got the question right.' There was a spontaneous murmur of agreement.

'I'm supposed to be retired now!' Hallie pouted unconvincingly. If she'd wanted to be unnoticed, she could have just stayed still. Hallie was a ham actress from away back. It was a wonder she hadn't gone on the stage. Or perhaps she had and had been too hammy to earn a living. A television quiz show was just about right for her.

'Well —' Hallie made them beg for it, Connie gave her that. She'd really learned to milk her applause during those weeks on television. 'Well, perhaps just this once . . .'

Then she was off again, in the famous back somersaults that, Connie suspected, had had so much to do with the Ordways winning the Grand Prize. The Quizmaster had practically fed them the answers on one programme Connie had caught. Not surprisingly. They had captured the imagination of the nation and the quiz show's ratings had zoomed; it would have taken a suicidally inclined Quizmaster to ring down the curtain on such a popular act.

I don't want to knock it, I just want to get in on it. The famous line crossed Connie's mind and she grimaced inwardly. If she and Cosmo could ever come up with a double act half as successful, they'd be set for life.

There was a fresh outburst of applause, this time from the doorway. The afternoon cinema showing had just let out and some of the audience had paused to take in this extra show.

Hallie, flushed and triumphant, held out her arms and took a deep bow.

'I think that's all, folks.' Connie dismissed her class. 'We won't try to follow that. It would just bring out all our inferiority complexes.'

Amid a ripple of laughter, the women dispersed. Hallie nimbly sidestepped a couple who wanted to speak to her and came over to Connie.

'Gee, I'm sorry,' she said. 'I didn't mean to break things up —'

'You didn't,' Connie said, not quite truthfully. She checked her watch. 'It's finishing time, anyway. I've got to shower and get changed for dinner.'

'Me too,' Hallie said. 'I'm glad we chose second sitting. I don't know how we'd manage, otherwise. The day just flies past.'

Even more so when you're working. Connie didn't say it. She gave Hallie a pleasant nod and started back towards her cabin. With luck, she might be able to snatch a quick cat nap before dinner.

And then on to the festivities of another glamorous night aboard the Empress Josephine, as the brochure said.

The telephone rang in the Purser's Office just as Carl Daniels was about to join his table for the second sitting. He listened incredulously to the Chief Electrician's voice, unable to take in what it was telling him.

'Would you repeat that, please?'

'I said, it's one hell of a mess.'

'Not that — the rest of it.'

'You heard. Three of them — all Nhumbalans. Stupid buggers thought they'd found a nice quiet place to sneak into and have a little party. We found a broken bottle of rum and a deck of cards scattered around the bodies —'

'Three bodies —' Daniels's throat was tight.

'More or less. What's left of them. They're not in very good shape. Of all places to choose — the bottom of a lift shaft!'

'The bottom of a lift shaft,' Daniels repeated dully.

'I suppose they thought it was safe there. That lift only operates mornings and evenings. No one ever uses it in the afternoons, so we put it out of action then. Either something went wrong and someone managed to get it working when it shouldn't have been, or they drank too much and fell asleep and were sitting down there at the bottom of the shaft when the lift went back into operation for the first sitting crowd. Either way, it's a hell of a mess down there.'

'I'll be along in a few minutes,' Daniels said reluctantly. 'As soon as I can make some arrangements about tonight.' He rang off and stood staring into space.

Thank heaven no passengers were involved. The traitorous thought crossed his mind before he could censor it. Three deaths were appalling, no matter who was involved. But there was no time to stand here thinking about it. He picked up the receiver again and dialled quickly.

'Pesky —' He'd been lucky and caught the Cruise Director before he left his cabin. 'Pesky, I'm sorry about this, but something urgent has come up —' His throat tightened and he had to swallow before he could continue.

'I can't explain right now — there isn't time — but could you take the horse-racing in the Main Lounge after dinner? There's a bit of an emergency. I'll tell you about it later . . . Thanks.' He locked up the office and strode boldly across the lobby, trying not to seem hurried.

Pesky was being awfully good about this sudden change of plan but he was probably resigned to the fact that it was going to be a difficult trip. Ordinarily, Waring would have taken the horse-racing and the bingo, as well as some of the other strain.

Waring . . . what could have possessed the Assistant Purser to jump ship without a word of explanation? If he had missed the sailing, there should have been a radio-telephone message of apology . . . It was as though something were trying to catch at Daniels's attention, but he had no time to think about it.

Damn Waring! Can't worry about him now. Not with that hellish accident to clear up. Damn the Nhumbalan regulations, which had foisted a quota of native crew on board ships allowed to fly their flag. Damn the owners of the Line, while he was at it, for registering in Nhumbala because it was the cheapest flag of convenience available — even if it wasn't so convenient for the ship and its officers.

At least it ought to be possible to keep news of the accident from the passengers. Two of the dead men had worked in the engine-room and one in the kitchen. The passengers had never seen them and would not miss them.

They'd have to hold the burial service at dawn before any of the passengers were stirring. It would all be over before anyone was awake.

All over before they reached Nhumbala. It was a politically sensitive area of the world and it would not be wise to sail into port with the crushed bodies of three of its citizens. There would be too many professional agitators ready to make capital out of an incident like that. They would turn the dead men into martyrs for their cause, symbols of the capitalist exploitation of their innocent recently-emergent nation, and all the other clichés of political claptrap the world had learned so well.

No, tip the poor stupid bastards over the side and sail away from the problem. Davy Jones's Locker was deep and wide, plenty of room for all . . .

He was jumpy, too jumpy. Why else would the hairs on the back of his neck suddenly prickle? *Someone was following him.* Ordinarily he wouldn't even have noticed. This evening he was so much on edge that he darted into one of the side passages lined with cabin doors and paused there until the follower went past.

But the footsteps slowed as they approached the opening . . . and halted. Ridiculously, Carl caught his breath, his muscles tightened, a flood of adrenalin coursed through him. *Fight or flight* — but flight was out of the question. He clenched his fists.

'Ah-ah-ah-*ah* . . .' The waggling finger appeared round the corner, followed by the foolish, witless face. '*That's* not the right way. *Been* down there. Nothing but cabins. Try again, ol' boy!'

It was that idiot drunk. Why did there have to be one — if not more — on every trip? Carl had spotted him first night out — he was hard to miss — and had kept tabs on him in a desultory way ever since. He appeared to be harmless. Except, perhaps, to himself. Although he was obviously going to be a great source of annoyance to innocent bystanders — like his tablemates. Fortunately he had a cabin to himself.

'Good evening, Mr —' Carl forced a smile, mentally flipping through the files of his memory until the name came to him — 'Mr Smithers.'

D. D. Smithers — that was the name. *D-and-D*, the staff had already dubbed him. *Drunk-and-Disorderly*. Predominately drunk, in these early days, but just give him time. The disorderly would undoubtedly follow. Perhaps the best thing to do would be to see that he was allowed to consume enough drink to knock him out for the remainder of the voyage. Or, at least, for the next few days.

'Three down —' D-and-D raised the relevant number of fingers and waggled them in his face — 'and three to go. Play the game, ol' boy. Fair's fair, right?'

'*Three!*' Forgetting himself, Daniels snatched for the man's collar. 'How do you know? Who told you?'

'Ah-ha!' D-and-D dodged the grasping hand. 'Caught you fair 'n' square this time. No' fair runnin' away 'n' disappearin' where the passengers can't go.'

'You said three —' Daniels would not let him evade the issue. 'What three were you talking about? How did you find out?'

'In the brochure. Promised six bars. Found three bars —' D-and-D seemed vaguely amazed that anyone could have questioned his meaning. 'Three more bars to go. Don'worry, I'll find them. With or without your help.'

'Bars!' Daniels forced a smile, uneasily aware of how close he had come to manhandling a passenger. 'Is that all?'

'What else is there?'

For him, nothing. It could be true, Daniels reflected, probably was true. His own nerves had nearly betrayed him into letting slip the secret that must be kept.

The passengers mustn't find out was the cardinal rule when anything went wrong on board. Death would upset them more than anything, even though they didn't know the crewmen involved. It was important to keep the fact secret.

'Wouldn't min' if you *did* help —'

A melodic ripple of chimes over the tannoy interrupted D-and-D. He raised his head questioningly, as though reminded of something.

'Second sitting, Mr Smithers,' Carl prompted. 'You'd better get along to your table.' In one smooth motion, he moved forward, side-stepped D-and-D and gained the clear corridor.

'Right. But —' The chimes rippled again, D-and-D lost track of his proposed argument. He turned in the direction of the dining-room and, when he turned back to add another comment, the ship's officer had disappeared.

'All right for you,' D-and-D muttered darkly. 'But I'll get you next time.'

CHAPTER 4

'If you ask me, this is a jinxed crossing.' Pesky Calhoun was the first to give voice to the gathering malaise. 'If I hadn't suspected it when I got my first look at the passengers, I'd know it for certain now.'

'All passengers look like that the first couple of days out,' Dr Parker said. 'In fact,' he added thoughtfully, 'I hardly ever see them looking any other way.'

'This crossing lasts too long.' Carl Daniels poured large and sympathetic drinks all round. It was too early in the day but they were all chilled and emotionally upset. 'With no shore excursions to keep the passengers amused, all they can do is dress up to try to impress each other. They're back and forth to my office like demented homing pigeons, taking their jewellery out of the safe to wear for dinner and putting it back after the last dance. To cap it all, Waring had to go and miss the ship. I've got to handle everything on my own.'

'Jinxed,' Pesky said gloomily. 'Jinxed from the outset. I told you so.'

Daniels poured him an extra large drink, too.

'Twenty tables of bridge, I ask you!' Pesky brooded. 'The card room only holds six tables. Who'd expect so many bridge nuts on this cruise? Don't ask me where we're going to put them.

I had a word with Jacques about screening off a corner of the dining-room between meals, but he went mad.'

'Let's not talk about cards.' Joan shuddered.

'Sorry, I guess it was association of ideas —' Pesky broke off. Wrong thing to say. Again.

They were gathered in the Purser's cabin, having just come from their grim duties on deck. In the dank and chill of dawn, with a pale grey light beginning to streak the horizon, they had committed the bodies of their shipmates to the deep. The fact that they had not known the men personally was immaterial. The solemnity of the age-old ceremony had struck deep into their innermost being, reminding them of their own mortality . . . and that the sea was always waiting.

'There's something strange about that card game,' Daniels said slowly. 'I mean, when I've seen the native crew playing cards, there were usually two or four of them. What game would they be playing three-handed?'

'Perhaps there were four originally,' Parker said. 'One of them might have gone off for another bottle of rum or to take a leak, and come back to find the lift on top of his chums. He wouldn't be anxious to report it, they don't volunteer much.'

'That they don't.' The Chief Engineer stared down into his drink. 'They didn't work much, either, but I'll miss the little buggers. No one should have died like that.'

'No . . .' Daniels hesitated, but he had to consider the passengers first and foremost. 'We'll be able to put the lift back into operation soon, won't we?'

'Oh, aye, today, if you like.' The Chief sighed heavily. 'No damage done to the machinery.'

'We'll do it, then,' Daniels decided. 'What passengers don't know, won't bother them. And there are always some who'll complain if their nearest lift isn't working.'

'There are some who'll complain about anything. I ought to be getting back to my post, I'm supposed to be on duty.' But Joan allowed Carl Daniels to pour more brandy into her glass. It had been her first funeral at sea — the first for most of them —

and she knew that it would haunt her dreams for the rest of her life. Right now, she was afraid of breaking down and crying, but the brandy was steadying her as it was intended to.

'They say things come in threes —' Pesky tried for a note of optimism. 'Let's hope the cycle is complete now.'

'It depends on how you're counting.' Parker was giving no comfort. 'The way I figure it, the suicides yesterday would count as one, this accident makes two . . . so we still have one more to come . . .'

'I'd rather not count it that way,' Pesky said. If this was a sample of the doc's bedside manner, no wonder he hadn't been able to make it on shore. 'The way I reckon, I'd count Waring's missing the ship as the first calamity.'

'I'm not sure you can count it that way.' Dr Parker would not be placated. 'The other incidents involved deaths — and Waring isn't dead. That we know of.'

Something prickled along Carl Daniels's spine. *That we know of* . . . but that was ridiculous. Or was it? Waring had always been a good officer. He had never missed a sailing before.

'Let's stop giving each other the heebie-jeebies.' Pesky's laugh was a good effort, but sounded rusty. 'Next thing, we'll be telling ghost stories. And I haven't got the time —' He glanced at his watch. 'It's my turn to pace the early joggers around the deck. So, if you'll excuse me . . .'

'That's right.' Joan stood, grateful that the gathering was breaking up. 'I must get back. My lot are probably screaming for their early morning tea . . .'

'It's about time! I've been ringing for half an hour. Where have you been?' Mrs Anson-Pryce glared at the stewardess.

'I'm sorry,' Joan said. 'I was attending to . . . other duties. What is it you want?'

'I want several things I can quite see I am unlikely to get on this ship! I want peace and quiet. I want prompt service. I want undisturbed sleep. These things don't seem too much to ask at the prices we're paying. I shall never travel on this ship again!'

'I'm sorry, madam,' Joan apologized automatically. 'Is there anything I can get for you now?'

'This is the noisiest ship I have ever been on.' Mrs Anson-Pryce had not finished complaining. 'First yesterday morning, and now this morning. Noise, noise, noise! Shouting, machinery grinding, things falling into the water — splash, splash, splash! What are you doing — jettisoning cargo?!'

Joan gasped and swayed. She caught at the life-jacket hatch to steady herself.

'Are you all right, girl? You've gone quite pale.' Mrs Anson-Pryce tossed back the duvet and swung her feet to the carpet.

'No, I'm all right.' Joan stepped back. They had not registered that Mrs Anson-Pryce's cabin was within earshot of the activities of the past two mornings. 'I — I don't know why you've been disturbed. I'm sure it won't happen again. If you like, I'll have a word with the Purser. Perhaps he could change you to a quieter cabin.'

'I'm settled in this one now,' Mrs Anson-Pryce said stubbornly. 'I hate chopping and changing about. I'm all unpacked. It's no holiday for me if I have to keep moving from one stateroom to another.'

'I'm sure it won't happen again,' Joan said desperately.

'Humph!' Mrs Anson-Pryce sniffed. Her eyes narrowed and she sniffed again — suspiciously.

Oh Lord — the brandy! Joan tried to hold her breath as Mrs Anson-Pryce advanced on her, still sniffing.

'Young woman, you've been drinking!' Mrs Anson-Pryce accused. 'At *this* hour — and when you're supposed to be in charge of passengers. It's disgraceful!'

'Yes, madam,' Joan said woodenly. There was no way she could explain it. She wasn't alert enough at the moment to dream up a good lie — and it would be unthinkable to tell a passenger the truth. It would get round the ship like wildfire.

'You rang, madam.' There was nothing to do but brazen it out. 'Did you want a cup of tea?'

'Coffee,' Mrs Anson-Pryce corrected. 'And you'd better get some for yourself, while you're about it!'

'Yes, madam.' Joan turned.

'I'll overlook it, this time,' Mrs Anson-Pryce called after her. 'But if I ever see you in this condition again, I shall go to the Captain immediately.'

Captain Falcon stretched out on his bunk with a contented sigh. It had been a good service. He hoped he'd get as good a one himself when his time came. He asked for nothing better than to be buried at sea himself. It was quick, clean and decent. Let the landlubbers shiver and talk about being eaten by fish. They let themselves be shut up in boxes, heavy earth piled on them, and then waited for the worms. Of the two, the fish were cleaner.

Nor did he mind the thought of being eaten by fish. He'd eaten enough of them. Turn and turn about in the pursuit of Nature's bounty. It was fair enough. A man ate more fish in his lifetime than he ate worms.

Captain Falcon relaxed, conscious of a job well done. He gave himself up to the lulling sway of the ship and his eyes began to close. He had no patience with passengers who complained of seasickness. Their minds weren't attuned to the infinite, that's all. How could they be sick on board a ship with the sea herself rocking it like a cradle? *Cradle of the deep.* That was what wise men called it.

For himself, he often thought that it was like lying atop a beloved, gently moving body. It was not a thought he voiced to others, of course. People might get the wrong idea.

The sea — from the cradle to the grave. What more could a man ask?

The crew were edgy all day. The passengers felt the uneasiness in the air and became obscurely disturbed. It made them more difficult than ever. It was the fourth day out and they had exhausted the delights of exploring the ship, marked out the narrow runs of their own territory, and were now looking for something to occupy their minds and prevent them from discovering that they were in danger of becoming bored.

Connie wound up her Keep-Fit Class with relief. They were no longer so enthusiastic about keeping fit, nor even attending. That suited her just fine, she'd be glad to drop the class if she thought she could get away with it. There was plenty else to do — for her, if not the passengers.

Hallie Ordway had slipped into the back row late — thank heaven. Hallie was a disruptive influence, even though she had shot her bolt at the beginning and was beginning to realize it. The other women had been willing to applaud the sideshow once, but they did not like being continually reminded that their own joints were stiffening and they carried too much weight. They would never be able to do cartwheels and back-flips again — if they had ever been able to do them, which was debatable.

Hallie was whispering something to Mary Lawton now, glancing towards 'teacher' like a naughty schoolgirl. That was probably about her mental level. It was too bad she was booked for the full cruise and would be returning from Nhumbala on the *Empress Josephine*. Connie already had the suspicion that a little of Hallie Ordway would go a long, long way.

'Ssst!' Cosmo stood in the doorway, gesturing to her in the Control Room language for 'Wind it up'. His stint with the skeet-shooters was over and they wanted to rehearse a couple of dance numbers for tonight's floor show in the Night Club.

She nodded and dismissed the class. He came out on the floor to join her. There was no other place with enough room, but she still wasn't happy about it. It was one thing to appear in the finished product, all rehearsed and polished performance. It was quite another to rehearse in public and make your mistakes with everyone looking on and — in Hallie's case — grinning broadly.

Hallie took a chair at the edge of the floor and leaned back, probably hoping the ship would lurch and they'd both fall on their faces. Mary Lawton took the chair beside her, although a swift glance at her watch suggested that she was not going to stay long. With luck, she might drag Hallie away for a drink before dinner.

Connie's eye was caught by a lone figure weaving along the perimeter of the dance floor. D-and-D — the nickname was inevitable, given his initials and proclivities. By now, most of the crew and staff had been buttonholed by him, waving his brochure and demanding directions to the sixth bar. In vain had everyone tried to explain that it was an old brochure and the sixth bar had been dispensed with when the ship had been refitted last season. D-and-D believed in cold print, not warm assurances. He was going to find that sixth bar or perish in the attempt. Good luck to him. He had already found too many bars in his lifetime, that was his trouble.

D-and-D paused and peered suspiciously under a table, then straightened, shaking his head. He turned and moved slowly and unsteadily out of sight, still searching for his phantom bar.

Well, that ought to keep him occupied for the voyage. It was nice when the passengers had a hobby.

'We ought to have a couple more rehearsals with Pesky,' Cosmo murmured in her ear. 'We've billed *Design for Living* for a matinee in the lecture theatre tomorrow and I'm sure he doesn't know half his lines.'

'He can write them on his cuffs,' Connie murmured back.

'His cuffs aren't big enough.'

'He can always ad lib. No one on this ship is likely to know the difference. Don't worry about Pesky. He'll manage.'

Pesky was taking a quiet turn around the Sports Deck. It was deserted now that the first sitting was in progress. This was the time of day he liked best, the only time when he had a few minutes to himself. He could turn off the beaming bonhomie and even let his face fall into mournful lines if he liked, just to give it a rest. There was no one to observe him.

He kicked a cartridge shell over the side as he walked along. Someone had been careless about cleaning up. He'd have a word with Daniels. The crew were pretty shaken by the accident

— as who wasn't? — but it didn't do to get sloppy. If routine wasn't followed and the ship kept in order, the passengers would begin to wonder why. And no one wanted to face any questions right now.

The wind was sharpening as the sun went down. Pesky stood at the bow rail for only a moment, during which the wind became cold and cutting, before turning his back on it and strolling to the aft rail. It was better there. He leaned his arms on the rail and looked out over the lower decks and the broad white wake of the ship's passage.

Somewhere out there the weighted tarpaulin shrouds were lying on the ocean floor. It didn't bear thinking about. Pesky turned his thoughts away, observing with approval the activity on the deck below.

The deckchair attendants had begun closing up shop for the night. They began at the deserted outer edges of the rows of deckchairs, collecting blankets and mattresses, a strong hint to the diehards still stubbornly occupying deckchairs that it was time to go below. There were always a few who held out until the very last moment, almost defying the attendants to roust them from the chairs they intended to occupy for the voyage.

A few of the more easily intimidated, however, tossed aside blankets and struggled to their feet. The hard core remained impervious to the power of suggestion.

The deck attendants moved into the second phase of their operation, gathering up each skeletal deckchair and folding it with the maximum amount of noise before tossing it on top of the growing pile with a loud clatter.

A few more passengers moved reluctantly. Now only four remained, laid out side by side in the centre of the middle row, shrouded in their blankets, silently defying the attempt to move them inside. Around them, the circle of empty deckchairs gradually diminished until they were lying in a little island of empty chairs.

The deck attendant looked up and, seeing Pesky, gave a hopeless shrug. Pesky nodded and waved acknowledgement.

The deckchair attendants, mindful of expected tips, could not harry their prospects beyond a certain point. If they wanted to lie there all night, it was their dubious privilege.

However, the Cruise Director could harry anyone — in fact, that was what he was paid for. Pesky turned and made his way swiftly down the narrow stairs to the lower deck. He was always hounding people to join in games and activities, it would surprise no one if he also threw them out of their deck chairs. Besides, it was growing late and they'd be equally annoyed if they slept through their dinner hour.

'Here we are — here we are —' He advanced on them determinedly, noting that the deckchair attendants had prudently disappeared, so as not to be associated with him. 'Look at all those lazybones!'

They didn't stir. Trying to ignore him, eh?

'No, you don't! he cried. 'It's that Pesky character again! Come to disturb your rest. Come on, now, it's nearly second sitting. You won't have time to change if you don't get moving now.'

No one moved. They remained obstinately huddled in their blankets, even though the air had now grown so chill that a second blanket must be needed to keep them comfortable.

What was this — some kind of passengers' strike?

'So you want to play it that way, do you?' He moved to stand at the foot of the deckchairs. 'You ought to know better by this time. You know that Pesky character never lets you rest in peace. I'll give you till the count of three, and then — off with your blankets! That will make you move!'

Still no response. Pesky shuddered suddenly in the icy wind.

'One . . . two . . . two-and-a-half —'

No one laughed.

'Okay, three!' He sprang forward. 'Here I come, ready or — *Jesus!*'

CHAPTER 5

'I don't know,' Cosmo Carpenter said desperately for the fourth time — once for each body. 'How am I supposed to know what happened?'

'Damn it, man!' Captain Falcon barked. 'You were supervising the skeet-shooting. You must have noticed who was there. You *must* have seen someone aiming in the wrong direction!'

'I didn't,' Cosmo said. 'I wasn't watching the guns. I was too busy releasing the traps. Everybody kept shouting that I wasn't fast enough.'

'But you must have noticed something —'

'I was too busy. Besides, people kept coming and going. Every time I opened my eyes there was someone new —' He broke off guiltily.

'What do you mean — opened your eyes?'

'I —' There was nothing for it, he had to confess the shameful truth. 'I hate guns. Every time one goes off, I have to shut my eyes. I couldn't have seen anything, anyway.'

'You . . . shut . . . your . . . eyes!' Captain Falcon closed his own eyes for a brief wistful daydream of an era when a Captain had been allowed a few simple pleasures, like keelhauling imbeciles. 'You shut your eyes!'

'Yes, sir.' Cosmo stood at attention, in no doubt that he was being court-martialled. Why hadn't he taken that summer repertory job at the Playhouse in Florida?

'It isn't fair —' Connie defended him. *That* was why he hadn't gone to Florida. There had been no job for her there. 'How was Cosmo supposed to know that somebody had such rotten aim? You ought to be more careful who you let go in for dangerous sports.'

Four dead bodies suggested something more sinister than an inept sportsman with rotten aim. An uneasy stir swept through the listeners in the cabin, but no one wanted to voice the alternative suggestion: *malice aforethought.*

It was unthinkable. These things don't happen. It was some sort of nightmare. And yet, there had to be a logical explanation.

But what? One shooting death could be an accident. Four in, literally, a row smacked of deliberation. Was there a madman on board? Some crazed sportsman setting his own targets?

'We can't give the passengers tests before turning them loose on the Sports Deck.' Captain Falcon answered Connie's complaint. 'We have to take their word for it,' he added regretfully, 'that they know what they're doing.'

'Well, you can't blame Cosmo,' Connie insisted stubbornly.

'Perhaps not.' The Captain had already come to that decision, with great reluctance. 'But how could this have happened? Someone must be to blame.'

Silence answered him.

'All right,' he said to Cosmo. 'Make out a list of as many who were shooting as you can remember and let me have it. Now stand down. I mean,' he corrected, 'sit down.'

'Yes, sir.' Cosmo collapsed into a chair before he could change his mind.

'What about it, Daniels?' Captain Falcon turned to the Purser. 'Can we keep the lid on this?'

'Just about,' Daniels said. 'The two women were sisters, Miss Agatha and Miss Arlene Christopherson. They shared a cabin and didn't circulate much. Only the people at their table are likely to notice they're missing. That won't be for a while. No one is every surprised if people miss a few meals at sea. I've been on the ship-to-shore to the next of kin, there's only a distant cousin. He's quite content to have them buried at sea —' It stuck in his craw, the way the cousin had jumped at the idea, realizing that it would save the cost of shipping the bodies home and a double burial on land. Although, with the cost of funerals, it was hard to blame him. 'Delighted, in fact.'

'So he should be. Only sensible thing to do. What of the others? They being reasonable, too?'

'Mr Preedy seems to have been alone in the world. No next of kin, only a bank to be notified in case of accident. I tried to get through, but there was no answer. Not banker's hours. I don't imagine they'll object to having him buried at sea.'

'And the other one?'

'Mrs Davis.' That was the one Daniels didn't want to think about. 'I spoke to a daughter. She was hysterical as soon as she realized what I was telling her. Refused permission, wants the body sent home, was babbling about an autopsy, lawsuit, criminal negligence, you name it. I thought perhaps Dr Parker could talk to her in a day or so, when she's had time to calm down.'

'Yes . . .' Captain Falcon sighed deeply. 'Well, one out of four isn't too bad. Could be worse. They might all have been trouble-makers. Parker, you'll deal with it?'

'I'll try.' Parker's tone left no doubt as to his opinion of his likely success. 'She doesn't need an autopsy to tell her the cause of death — even I can tell her that, with no probing or dissection needed. It was a gunshot wound. They all were. What I can't tell her is who did it. And no shore-based doctor or lawyer will be able to tell her that, either.'

'We'll find out.' Captain Falcon did not admit the possibility of failure. 'We're all cooped up aboard this vessel for six more days before we hit port. We're bound to sort it out by then.'

'What do you mean — Table Six?' Mrs Anson-Pryce's eyes blazed as dangerously as her diamonds, reminding everyone in sight that she possessed power backed with limitless funds. One crossed her at his peril.

'Just for tonight, ma'am,' Pesky Calhoun temporized hastily, wishing he were somewhere else — anywhere else. 'Your friends weren't . . . um . . . *aren't* feeling well. Maybe they'll be back to normal by tomorrow night.'

'Nonsense!' She glared at him indignantly. 'The Misses Christopherson are not susceptible to seasickness. They once sailed round the Cape of Good Hope during a hurricane. They told me so last night. They can't possibly be ill.'

Pesky shrugged, the apologetic smile frozen on his face, while inwardly he seethed. *Why did they have to be bridge players?* Now he was left with half a table. *And why, oh why, did they have to be at Mrs Anson-Pryce's table?* The remaining woman at the table had been a quiet little creature who had meekly acquiesced in his suggestion that she might prefer watching the film tonight. He'd known there'd be trouble with Mrs Anson-Pryce and it had taken a faster shuffle than a Mississippi riverboat gambler had ever produced to persuade another meek character at Table Six that he didn't look too well this evening and would be better off having an early night, and then sliding Mrs Anson-Pryce into his place at the table. It was only a short-term solution, but it would give him time to try to sort something out for the rest of the voyage.

And yet, Mrs Anson-Pryce was complaining! Of course, she couldn't know how much trouble he'd gone to on her behalf. God forbid that she ever find out why the change was necessary.

'If you don't sit in —' he had a sudden inspiration — 'then Table Six will be short-handed and won't be able to play.'

'Oh, well . . .' Thus appealed to, Mrs Anson-Pryce allowed herself to be persuaded. 'This is most unsatisfactory, however. I trust it won't happen again.'

'So do I!' Pesky said fervently. 'I mean, we'll do everything we can to get back to normal as soon as possi —' That wasn't right, either. It suggested the Misses Christopherson were suffering from something it was possible to remedy.

'What?' Mrs Anson-Pryce glanced at him suspiciously. There was something wrong about his statement and his attitude, but she could not quite put her finger on it.

'Just come with me,' Pesky said hastily. 'I'll introduce you to Table Six. I'm sure you'll like them. They're very nice people.'

Mrs Anson-Pryce followed him over to the table where a man was nervously and not very expertly shuffling cards. The woman sitting opposite the empty chair was drumming her fingers impatiently on the table, sending out sparks of dancing light from the diamond rings on almost every finger.

The woman sitting opposite the dealer smiled a timid welcome as Pesky led Mrs Anson-Pryce to the table. The woman's jewellery was more subdued but equally impressive. Rich lustrous pearls gleamed at her throat and ears; in addition to a plain gold wedding ring, she wore only a small diamond and ruby ring, the sort of thing a young couple bought for an engagement ring before growing rich enough to afford pearls and winter cruises.

'Mr and Mrs Burke —' Pesky introduced — 'Mrs Morton, Mrs Anson-Pryce is going to make up your table tonight. I'm sure you'll . . . um . . .' He backed away, making social noises and escaped quickly.

'Do sit down.' The woman opposite the empty chair stopped drumming and surveyed Mrs Anson-Pryce with a cool assessing stare, then leaned forward more cordially, diamond ear-rings swinging. 'I'm Madge Morton,' she said. 'I'm American. I hope you don't mind my saying so, but you've got some really lovely diamonds there, dear. My late husband owned a chain of jewellery shops — and I ought to know.'

'Oh, yes?' Mrs Anson-Pryce raised her eyebrows and allowed herself a small superior smile. 'I'm South African. *My* late husband owned a diamond mine.'

'You're hiding from me —' The voice halted Pesky in mid-flight down the covered Promenade Deck.

'Oh, good evening, Mr Smithers. I didn't see you.' He ground his teeth behind his smile.

'You're shtill hiding it from me —' D-and-D swayed playfully in front of him, waggling a finger in reproach. 'Not fair, ol' boy, not fair, y'know.'

'Honestly, Mr Smithers, I assure you, if I knew where it was, I'd tell you.'

'Aah-ha! That's what *you* say —'

Was the ship rolling, or was it just D-and-D? Pesky grappled with his emotions. If he straight-armed the damned drunk and made his escape, would D-and-D remember it and bring him to book before the Captain later? Or was he so drunk he wouldn't remember it ten seconds later?

'Says right *here* —' D-and-D pulled a tattered brochure from his pocket and waved it in Pesky's face. '*Empress Josephine* has shix bars on board for the delic — delli — for the passengers. Only found five, so far. *Got* to be another round here shomewhere.'

'You'd think so, wouldn't you?' Regretfully Pesky decided that someone so insistent upon his rights in the matter of drinking holes would be only too likely to remember and report any failings on the part of the staff. He'd have to play it another way.

'Where *is* it, then? That's all I'm asking. Doesn't seem too much to ask. What you're here for, isn't it? Where is it?'

'Not too far.' Pesky took a deep breath, put a tentative hand on D-and-D's shoulder and turned him round. 'You go down to the end of this corridor, turn left until you come to the frammis by the ogglyway, then take the stairs up to the half-landing and turn right and go straight down as far as the crudgin. Turn left there, then right at the drenkidge, left, left, then straight ahead you'll see the entrance. You can't miss it. Now, have you got that?'

'Perf'ly clear.' D-and-D nodded bemusedly. 'Thank you, ol' boy. Nice to know theresh somebody aboard this ship who knows his business.'

'You're welcome.' Pesky gave him as hard a push as he dared to start him tottering down the corridor. The old double-talk routine worked every time with drunks. They never wanted to admit they were too drunk to understand what you were saying. 'Remember, you can't miss it.'

'Never missed a bar yet,' D-and-D assured him weaving away.

'I believe it,' Pesky said under his breath, wrestling with bitter thoughts. Why couldn't a useless lush like that have got in the way of a stray bullet instead of the respectable citizens who had?

The midnight show had just started in the Night Club. Cosmo was warming up the crowd, or trying to. Not that there was much of a crowd. Not that he was in a mood to fight their resistance. If they didn't want to laugh, why should they? He didn't feel like laughing himself. The difference was that he knew the reason why.

But the audience knew something, or suspected. It was too early for passengers to have found out what had happened, but Cosmo didn't believe the Captain could keep the lid on this one. *Four* of them dropping out of sight? There must be questions, rumours, speculation. If an accident like that had happened in a theatre, it could never be kept quiet. And a ship in mid-ocean was even more of an enclosed world filled with cliques and temporary alliances.

But . . . *The Show Must Go On . . . Laugh, Clown, Laugh* . . . and all that. He wished he could laugh off the memory of Captain Falcon's face when he'd had to admit that he shut his eyes when the guns went off. Probably some day he'd be able to. In forty or fifty years, it would probably be a dining-out story, one of his party pieces. Reporters would love it when he was a Grand Old Man of the Theatre granting interviews. Probably.

He closed his eyes in agonized remembrance, automatically continuing with his patter, bridging the gap until Connie appeared and helped take some of the strain.

'And then there were these two drunks walking along a railroad track —' He hadn't intended to tell that one, hadn't thought of it in years, but it seemed suitable tonight.

'One drunk said to the other drunk, "This is the longest flight of stairs I've ever seen in my life." And the other one said, "I don't mind the stairs, but this low handrail is killing me." '

The wave of laughter swept over him, shocking his eyes open. It was the most positive response he'd had all evening. Then he saw why.

Old Drunk-and-Disorderly, already a familiar ship's character to everyone, stood swaying in the doorway. That must have
been why the old joke had come into his mind; his subconscious
must have registered the fact just before he closed his eyes and,
traitorously, flipped the joke to the tip of his tongue. And
everyone in the audience thought he'd done it deliberately.

D-and-D must think so, too. He stood frowning into the
room. The only person clearly visible in it was Cosmo, caught in
the spotlight.

*Connie, where are you? Never mind waiting for the cue — I need you
now!*

Wait until the Captain heard this one. Insulting passengers
to their face — in front of an audience. That would be rated
nearly as bad as letting them get killed.

Then Connie was beside him. Two against the world. Against
the audience. He looked down at her lovingly and hoped she
wouldn't be caught up in his punishment when the Captain
decided to toss him over the side and sail away.

Connie smiled out at the audience and they loved her. How
could they help it? She gave a little shuffling tap dance, nudging
Cosmo along with her over to the piano. Cosmo sank down on
the piano bench with relief, his trembling legs didn't have to
hold him up any more.

'All right, folks, time for a change of pace.' He smiled out at
the now-receptive audience. 'It's getting late, we're feeling
sentimental, so how about a few midnight melodies?'

Connie leaned back against the piano, Thirties-style, and let
her small sweet voice ripple out on cue:

'*Blue moon, you saw me standing alone . . .*'

From the doorway, D-and-D gave them a thumbs-up signal
and lurched away into the night. How much would he remember in the morning? Would he complain to the Captain?

Cosmo felt the onset of a familiar gnawing anxiety which was

not going to go away. If the Captain heard about this, he'd be a
dead duck.

Captain Falcon had troubles of his own. He stared down
incredulously at the note the Purser had handed to him.

'Where did you say you got this?'

'It was pushed under the grille in my office.' Pushed well
under and across the counter so that it couldn't be fished out
again by prying curious fingers and read by some unauthorized
person. It happened sometimes with bored, nosey passengers. 'I
found it just before midnight.'

'Before midnight . . .' Captain Falcon muttered abstractedly.
He had already glanced at the first two lines. He didn't like
them. He didn't want to go on reading. He knew he wasn't going
to like the rest of it any better.

'Yes, sir.' Carl Daniels was patient. Eventually the Captain
would have to stop stalling and read the note. Then the
responsibility would have been passed on. As much as it could
be. This was something none of them was going to be able to
escape. *The buck stops here.*

They locked gazes, each of them knowing what the other was
thinking. Fearing.

'I don't like this,' Captain Falcon said.

'Read it. You'll like it even less.'

Captain Falcon sighed deeply. He began to read. There was
no salutation. It began abruptly:

One might have been left behind.
Two might have had a suicide pact.
Three could have been an accident.
Doesn't four make you think?
Tomorrow, there'll be five.
Unless . . .

'Unless? Unless?' Captain Falcon turned the paper over.
Blank. He scrabbled in the envelope. Empty. 'Unless what?' He
raised his head to glare accusingly at Daniels.

'Where's the rest of it?'

'That's all there is.' Daniels met his eyes squarely. 'I've looked. Everywhere. That's all there is.'

'It can't be!' Captain Falcon shook the piece of paper frantically, as though it might subdivide and divulge the remainder of the message. 'It can't be!'

'It is.' Daniels let him worry the sheet of paper and envelope until the truth penetrated.

'Then . . . ?' Captain Falcon glanced at his watch. 'It's after one a.m. You said you got this before midnight. It says *tomorrow*. That means *today* . . . ?' He looked at Daniels appealingly. 'Doesn't it?'

'I'm afraid so, sir.'

'But . . . but . . .' His mind balked. 'What are we supposed to do? How can we stop it? Where are the instructions?'

'There aren't any, sir.' Daniels was pale and perspiring. He had been giving the problem all his attention. There was only one conclusion to be reached.

'But . . . ?'

'He doesn't intend us to be able to do anything about it. Not yet . . .'

Captain Falcon lowered the letter and stared at him, shaking his head in negation of a truth he already recognized.

'He doesn't mean us to have a chance to stop him. Either it's a hoax, in which case nothing will happen. Or else, he's going to kill five more people aboard this ship today — just to prove his power over us.'

CHAPTER 6

'That's the position.' Haggard, Captain Falcon faced the full muster of the *Empress Josephine* at an unprecedented emergency meeting. 'We can't be certain that it isn't some sort of hoax; we can't be sure that it is. I'm telling you this so that you can be on your guard. Whoever it is knows an uncomfortable amount about what has been going on. It's possible that we have a genuine threat. We must treat it as though it is.

'The pattern so far has been —' He cleared his throat. 'First, a member of the crew . . .' Waring wouldn't be catching up with the ship at Nhumbala, after all.

'Next, two of the passengers. Then, three of the crew. Lastly, four of the passengers . . .' He paused while an uneasy stir swept through his audience.

'I see you're with me —' He swept them with a keen look, as though searching out the weak links in the chain. 'On form, the next victims are scheduled to be five of the crew. Of yourselves, ladies and gentlemen . . .' He paused until the buzz of horror and excitement subsided.

'I want every one of you to be on your guard; to trust no one; to protect each other as well as yourselves. We are dealing with a maniac. Ten people on board this vessel may have been murdered already. We don't know why. Five more of you are in danger right now. I can't explain it. I can only ask you to be on the alert every moment. If you see anything at all suspicious — or even unusual — I would ask you to report it immediately to one of your officers, or to me personally. I cannot emphasize too strongly the importance of this . . .'

The rustle did not quite subside; the words of reservation had failed to provide as much comfort as intended. Sidelong glances betrayed that they were as ready to mistrust each other as any of the passengers.

'Needless to say,' Captain Falcon continued sternly, 'the passengers are not to know. We don't want panic aboard. We've got to keep this thing under control —'

'But, please, sir —' One of the Nhumbalans interrupted. No discipline, any of them. And this was supposed to be one of the best — so good that he had been promoted to serve in the dining-room. Not at any of the important tables, of course, but it was a step up to be a dining-room steward at all.

'Please, sir,' he insisted, 'there must be something else we can do. We must not just stand by tamely while the slaughterer walks among us.'

There was a frightened whimper from one of the Nhumbalan girl croupiers who were huddled together at one side.

'Emotive language won't help the situation, Edgar.' Damn the man — he'd panic the crew. 'We're going to do all we can. We want the rest of you to carry on normally and keep your eyes open. This may be only a bluff —' He broke off, realizing no one was going to believe that. They had just returned from seeing three bodies slide over the side. The killer wasn't bluffing.

'Right!' Captain Falcon nodded his head decisively. 'All officers remain for further instructions. The rest of you are dismissed.'

This was ridiculous! Joan pulled herself up sharply, realizing that she had just looked over her shoulder three times in a dozen steps. Why didn't she put her back to the wall and edge along crabwise?

It took her a moment to fight down the temptation to do just that. Her nerves were definitely fraying.

So were everybody else's nerves. Whose wouldn't be, knowing they were carrying a homicidal maniac on board? Not knowing how to identify him, or where and when he would strike again.

That wasn't quite true. They knew when he planned to strike again: today.

They had to find him first. Not so easy when there were over five hundred passengers, with the usual varying degrees of eccentricity, some so faceless and colourless that one hardly noticed their presence. Did madness lurk behind a nondescript façade? Or was it the final stage on the road to eccentricity?

She wished this corridor weren't quite so long and that there weren't so many turnings leading to the outside cabins. While she was at it, she might as well wish she wasn't on the ship at all. That she had missed the sailing — like Waring.

Only Waring hadn't — not through his own fault. The cold chill swept over her again. Waring had been the first to die. They had realized it after reading that terrible letter. All the while they had been grumbling about him and complaining about the extra work, he was lying . . . where? *Full fathom five* . . . ?

She shuddered and took a deep breath. She must look like a ghost. She'd frighten the life out of any passenger who met her. Worse, she might start them wondering what was wrong. Members of the crew were supposed to look calm and confident. It might be understandable to be terror-stricken; it would be unforgivable to look it.

She turned a corner with only the slightest hesitation and went up the semi-concealed staircase to the next deck.

The *Empress Josephine* was a one-class ship, but some cabins were classier than others. This section would be First Class, if there were one. As it was, the most expensive staterooms were situated here and both luxury suites. One suite was occupied by Herr Otto von Schreiber and his wife, the other had been part of the Grand Prize on *The Loot of a Lifetime*. The Ordways had spread out across it happily, the beginning of the luxury to which they were about to become accustomed.

Mrs Anson-Pryce was in the luxury stateroom next to the Ordway suite. Two of the other staterooms were unoccupied. Surprisingly, the remaining stateroom belonged to D-and-D Smithers. It was obviously worth almost any amount to his family to keep him a good distance away from themselves. He was a remittance man *de luxe*.

Joan sighed. She had all the fun people in her section this crossing.

She tapped perfunctorily at the door of the von Schreiber suite; they ought to be at second sitting breakfast now. There was no answer and she entered. The sitting-room was deserted and she moved on to the bedroom to make up the berths. She was dismayed to find Frau von Schreiber still lying abed and watching her with mournful accusing eyes.

'I'm sorry —' Joan began to back out. 'I'll come back later. I didn't realize —'

'*Nein*. Come in. It is all right.'

'You're not feeling ill?' Joan advanced into the room. 'Can I do anything?'

'I sleep late, that is all.' Frau von Schreiber sighed. 'I do not like to tell her, but that one at our table is right. There is much noise. Splash, splash, splash. I hear it too, only Otto says we must not give her the satisfaction that we agree. She is already too much above herself.'

'Oh dear! I'm so terribly sorry you've been disturbed.' Joan apologized automatically. 'I'm sure it won't happen again —' She broke off. *Tomorrow morning there'll be five . . . unless . . .*

'Do you think perhaps a whale follows this ship? Such splashes! If it is so big a whale, perhaps it may turn us over? Or maybe butt a hole in our side and sink us!'

'I'm sure nothing like that could happen.' Joan could be truthful and reassuring on that one point, if no other. 'I certainly haven't seen any whales about. Anyway, they couldn't damage a ship this size.'

'That is what Otto says.' Frau von Schreiber sat up, reviving under the comforting assurances. She looked at her watch. 'Such a pity. I have not time to dress and get to the dining-room. I shall have missed breakfast now.'

'I can bring you something.' Joan gave an inward sigh. She had been neatly trapped. 'What would you like, some coffee and croissants?'

'*Ja* — und orange juice und sausages und eggs. Und perhaps those pecan rolls mit strawberry jam —'

'I'll see to it right away.' Joan escaped hastily before Frau von Schreiber could further demonstrate her total recall of the breakfast menu.

The guns had been locked away and any prospective sportsman who inquired was to be told that the supply of ammunition had been found to be faulty and shooting was suspended for the remainder of the crossing.

Another suspected danger zone was the swimming pool. Two crew members were detailed to begin painting the railings near the pool and to keep a protective watch over the swimmers and sunbathers — and each other.

The three girl croupiers in the Casino had complained to the Purser that they felt the darkness of the casino put them at risk. They might be right. The roulette table, the blackjack table and the poker-dice table were small islands of light in a sea of gloom surrounded by looming fruit machines. The sheltered womblike atmosphere was psychologically sound for coaxing money out of the gamblers, but there was more than that to worry about now. Carl Daniels ordered full lighting for the casino tonight.

Below decks, the crew was divided. Some thought it was safer to walk alone rather than keep together in obliging little clusters, the better to be picked off *en masse*. Others clung to the theory of safety in numbers and moved in pairs and trios, watchful and foreboding.

The officers, on public view, had no choice. They opted to keep moving on endless tours of inspection. Wherever they went, they were alert for possible trouble. Such vigilance occasionally brought unexpected surprises.

'He's carrying a knife, Carl.' Jacques, the *maitre d'*, pushed the surly Nhumbalan dining-room steward into the Purser's Office ahead of him. 'A real pig-sticker!'

'It is for self-defence,' Edgar said. 'I will not be killed without a struggle. I kill him instead.'

'There'll be no more killing.' Daniels held out his hand. 'Let's have it.'

'I do not leave myself undefended!' Edgar crossed his arms and stared back defiantly.

'You're not undefended —' It would not only be undignified to lay hands on Edgar, it would be unpolitic. Edgar was some sort of relation to the despot currently ruling Nhumbala. It was all right for Jacques to have scuffled with him, but if a ship's officer got rough, it could cost them their flag of convenience. The owners of the shipping line would not be happy about that. 'We'll look after you.'

'As you looked after the others?'

That was unanswerable, but Daniels tried. 'We know what we're facing now. We're prepared.'

'*I* am prepared.' Edgar shook his head. '*You* are not.'

Jacques advanced half a step and gave Carl Daniels a meaningful look. Daniels shook his head. It wasn't worth the struggle. An Edgar disarmed would be an Edgar sulking in corners nourishing a grudge against the world and particularly against the officers of the *Empress Josephine*. They needed every man arrayed on their side against the unknown right now.

Anyway, what good would it do to confiscate the knife? Working in the dining-room, Edgar had free access to carving knives, shish kebab skewers and a whole assortment of lesser blades. He would replace the weapon before he'd been out of the office five minutes.

A carillon of bells rippled over the tannoy, announcing the first sitting for lunch and giving them all an honourable out.

'Back to your posts,' Daniels ordered. 'And be damned careful with that weapon, Edgar. We've had enough deaths on this ship.'

Cosmo Carpenter fitted a cigarette into a long silver holder and struck a mannered pose while, deep in his heart, he contemplated murder.

'But, darling . . .' Pesky Calhoun gave a careless laugh and a toss of his head. 'Oh, *but darling* . . .' He floundered there, waiting for someone to toss him a prompt or, better still, his next entire speech.

Fortunately, the audience was not over-familiar with the work of The Master — if they could recognize any of it at all in this truncated version. Possibly fifteen '*darlings*' in the space of three minutes sounded all right to them. They had been warned in the ship's newspaper that it was a Period Piece. But if Pesky couldn't manage to deliver a few more varied lines, even the dimmest of them was going to begin to smell a rat. A rat named Pesky Calhoun.

Connie did her best to throw him a lifeline, but it went over his empty head.

'Oh, darling!' The inane laugh rattled out again.

'*I'll kill him*,' Cosmo muttered to Connie under cover of lighting his cigarette with a flourish.

'*You'll have to get in line*,' she muttered back.

'Oh —' Pesky said, on a note of happy discovery. They looked at him hopefully. Had he remembered one of his lines at last?

'Oh, my dears!' No, he had just thought of a variation. '*My dears!*'

'Okay, so I was a little under-rehearsed,' Pesky said as the bewildered audience filed out. They had not prolonged the curtain calls. 'I'm sorry. I'll do better for tomorrow's matinee.'

'You needn't bother,' Cosmo said bitterly. 'If word gets around, we won't have an audience tomorrow and you won't need to worry about your performance.'

'Look, we've all got more to worry about today than some stupid script,' Pesky said.

'It wasn't stupid until you got at it!' Connie flew to Cosmo's defence. He'd cut and rearranged the play himself. 'You ruined the whole performance!'

'I said I was sorry.' Pesky looked forlorn. 'I'm usually better than that, honest, I am. But don't forget — I was the one who found those bodies yesterday.' He shuddered. 'You don't know what a thing like that can do to a guy.'

'I'm sorry,' Cosmo said into the momentary silence. 'Look, it wasn't really that bad. You just need a bit more rehearsal. Suppose we take over the cinema tonight after we finish in the Night Club. Connie and I will work with you on the sticky patches. No one will disturb us there and we can get in a couple of hours' work.'

'Great,' Pesky said eagerly. 'I'll read my lines over a few more times and I'll be word-perfect by tonight. I promise you.'

'Sure you will,' Cosmo said. Connie nodded. Neither of them believed it for a moment.

Captain Falcon hated the Captain's Cocktail Party and he was doomed to give two of them on each crossing; one for the first sitting and one for the second. Some ships divided the passenger list in half alphabetically, but it was easier for the dining-room staff to do it according to sittings. Things being as they were these days, it was getting as important to keep the crew happy as the passengers. Perhaps he should have settled for being captain of a little tramp steamer plying between tropical islands. Perhaps, if the situation aboard got any worse, he'd wind up doing that yet.

Dining-room stewards were dotted strategically around the Main Lounge, some bearing trays of canapés; some balancing trays of drinks: Martinis, Manhattans and champagne cocktails on each tray. Passengers who requested anything else would be accommodated, but most settled quite happily for what was on display.

Outside the closed curtained doors, passengers were already swarming, waiting for the moment the doors were flung back and the party began. *They* always seemed to enjoy it.

'Please —' Pesky Calhoun called out. 'Please form the reception line now. Captain, I'll introduce them to you, you pass them on to First Mate Hanson, he'll introduce them to Dr Parker, and the Purser will end the line and offer them drinks from the waiter standing behind him. Then they'll pass into the Main Lounge and they can talk to each other.'

Captain Falcon allowed himself to be nudged into position, feeling more like a sacrificial lamb than master of a ship. He checked that the reception line was in order, then turned to Pesky and grudgingly nodded.

'Here we go —' Pesky swung open the door and braced himself against the onslaught. 'Good evening, Mrs Morton, how very nice you look. Captain Falcon, Mrs Morton.'

'Madge Morton,' she gushed. 'I'm so pleased to meet you, Captain, you have such a lovely ship and I want to —'

'Thank you.' Captain Falcon flinched as the diamond rings dug into his hand. 'First Mate Hanson . . .' Expertly he passed her along the line. He closed his eyes momentarily to try to recover from the dazzle. Dark glasses should be part of the dress uniform on occasions like this.

Glittering occasions, as the brochure so aptly termed them. Some of these women were wearing jewels on almost every available surface. As the twittering passengers filed past, he noted that at least one trendy lady had taken a leaf from another culture and wore a diamond in one nostril. It was a wonder more of them didn't take it up as an opportunity to flaunt one more gem. He hated to think where else the trendy lady might hang a diamond or two if the opportunity occurred. He had never quite recovered from the day in an exotic port when, as a young man, he had seen a sign announcing: 'Ears, noses and nipples pierced.'

The ship's hairdressing salon, he saw, had done well out of the occasion, as usual. Presumably, the ship's Bijou Jewellery Boutique would also do well tomorrow, after some of the ladies had looked around and decided they were under-ornamented in comparison to the better arrayed passengers. One way and another, the shops did nearly as well as the casino on these long crossings, aided by the fact that the passengers had no shore excursions to distract their attention and siphon off their spending money.

'Mr and Mrs Ordway, but of course you know them already. They're at your table —'

'Hhrrmph! Yes, very busy this trip, unfortunately —' It was as close to apologizing as Captain Falcon ever went. 'But I'll be joining you tonight, after the cocktail party . . .' He passed them on hastily to the First Mate.

'Mr and Mrs von Schreiber — also at your table.' Pesky threw out the cue, realizing from the earlier reaction that

Captain Falcon had not yet been persuaded to grace his table with his presence.

'Tonight —' the Captain promised. Another drawback of these parties was that they were where his sins caught up with him. He was under special orders to give the 'full treatment' to the Ordways because they were the big quiz show winners and it would be good publicity. The von Schreibers were also down for the full treatment, but the reason was unspecified. Presumably they were of some importance in their own territory and good publicity from them would also be valuable.

The line filed past in a blur of monotony after that, until Captain Falcon heard Pesky groan.

'Oh no,' Pesky muttered under his breath. 'Not this!' He forced a welcoming smile. 'Good evening, Mr Smithers, I see you found your invitation —'

' 'Sright.' D-and-D swayed happily in the doorway, peering into the Lounge. 'Found the sixshth bar. Knew it had to be around here shomeplace.' He reeled forward towards a dark blur with an imposing air. 'Goo'evenin', bartender. I'll have a —'

'No, no, Mr Smithers —' Pesky hissed, snatching him back. 'That's the Captain! Captain Falcon,' he said, 'this is Mr Smithers. He's not at your table,' he added hastily.

'Hrrrm.' Captain Falcon hurtled D-and-D along the reception line with such force that he wound up shaking hands with the Purser, missing the two in the middle completely.

'Nice to see you, Mr Smithers,' Carl lied hospitably. 'May I offer your a drink?'

'Ver' kind.' D-and-D surveyed the offerings, then took a Martini in one hand and a Manhattan in the other. No one blinked an eyelash. He would be mixing gin and bourbon, but presumably his system was well-attuned to shocks of that nature.

As he reeled away, he collided with Edgar, who whirled about, simultaneously balancing his tray on one hand and reaching for his knife with the other.

'Stop it, Edgar!' Carl got to him just in time. 'Mr Smithers just lost his footing, that's all.' He had been perilously close to losing more than that.

Edgar muttered darkly in his own language and glared at the offending passenger before turning away. D-and-D wandered off, happily unconscious of what might have been his fate.

Carl Daniels rejoined the reception line, aware that he was beginning to tremble. That had been closer than he liked—and in full view of the entire party. It could have been a nasty scandal.

'Easy does it,' Dr Parker murmured. 'We'll all on edge.'

'But we're not all carrying knives.'

'So that was it!' Parker whistled softly. 'That's bad. The way things are, those maniacs could wind up murdering each other. Doing the killer's work for him.'

'Innocent people could get killed. More innocent people.'

'You need a drink. This looks like the end of the line coming up. We can play with one of these concoctions while we circulate for a while, then disappear and find an honest drink.'

'I'd rather stay here.' Carl looked around uneasily. 'Keep an eye on things. Make sure nothing —'

There was a babble of excitement on the far side of the lounge. Carl saw that a woman in the middle of a crowd had given a couple of yelps and thrown her hands into the air. What now? He started forward.

'Please —' Pesky pushed past him and covered the distance in a broken-field sprint. 'Please, Mrs Ordway — not here! There isn't room enough!'

There was a murmur of disappointment from the spectators who had been egging her on. Most of them were unfamiliar faces, but Pesky was used to the phenomenon by now. There were always a good sprinkling of people at the Captain's Cocktail Party who had never been seen before and — with luck — would never be seen again. Where they kept themselves the rest of the time, he neither knew nor cared. The problem now was that they had never before seen Hallie Ordway in live action and were urging her to do her stuff.

'Why don't we go out on deck?' Pesky beamed at all and sundry. 'There's plenty of room out there and we won't get in anybody's way.'

'It's raining,' Hallie Ordway pouted.

It was. Pesky hadn't had time to notice, but at some point during the late afternoon a drizzle had turned into a steady tropical downpour.

'Well —' he temporized. 'Well, why don't we adjourn to the gymnasium?'

'There's not enough room in there to swing a cat,' Hallie protested. 'It's full of all those stupid exercise machines. I could break my back if the ship rolled.'

'Oh —' Pesky tried to keep the wistful note out of his voice. 'Oh, we couldn't have that! Why don't we, say, take over the Lounge here tomorrow morning, after the Language Lesson? Maybe Mrs Ordway would be kind enough to go through her paces then — and we can all admire her.'

'I may not be in the mood then.' Hallie obviously wanted to be coaxed. 'Not the way I am right now.'

Then we'll wave a few dollar bills in front of your face. Pesky bit back the comment and tried to look suitably chastened.

'But, Mrs Ordway, we've *all* been hoping that you'd favour us with a demonstration —'

'Mrs Ordway —' Pesky felt himself shouldered aside and welcomed the interruption.

'Mr and Mrs Ordway —' The Purser appeared smiling before them. 'Captain Falcon's compliments. He'd like you to join him for a drink. If you'd just come this way . . .'

He was a wreck, Pesky told himself as he slowly descended the final flight of stairs to the cinema. He ought to take a hot bath and go to bed. Instead, he was condemned to a couple of hours of rehearsal for a show that only had two more performances anyway. He must have been mad to agree to the idea.

The Captain's Cocktail Party had run late, as usual. All right for the passengers, but it meant he'd had to bolt his dinner because the first sitting passengers were already waiting impatiently for their evening bingo game. Needless to say, he hadn't had a moment to glance at his lines.

He heard footsteps behind him. Suddenly he realized what fools they were, coming down to the darkened cinema all by themselves. With a homicidal maniac loose on board and sworn to despatch five members of the ship's company. How did he get himself into situations like this anyway?

The footsteps behind him hesitated, as though someone else might be thinking the same thing.

'Pesky?' Connie called out uncertainly.

'Right ahead of you.' Pesky leaned against the wall with relief. He'd expected them to be there ahead of him, but they were coming down the stairs behind him.

'You know,' Connie said, as they caught up to him, 'maybe this wasn't such a good idea, after all. It's kind of spooky down here.'

'It will be all right when we get some lights on,' Cosmo said. 'There are three of us. Don't worry, Pesky and I won't let anything happen to you.'

'That's right.' Pesky pushed open the door and stumbled into the blackness of the auditorium. He groped his way to the side aisle and led them down it and up on to the stage. He fumbled at the side panel in the wings for the footlights.

'Oh!' Connie blinked in the sudden brightness.

'Come on,' Cosmo said. 'Centre stage and take it from Act One, Scene One. The curtain rises . . .'

Connie walked centre stage, turned to face the empty chairs — and screamed.

'Who's out there?' Cosmo advanced to the footlights, staring out into the audience.

Five silent figures sat side by side in the front row.

'Oh Jesus!' Pesky said. 'Jesus — not again!'

'Come on, let's go see.' Cosmo caught his arm and pulled him to the steps. 'You stay there, Connie!'

'Can't I stay too?' Pesky pleaded. 'I've done this routine once.'

Relentlessly Cosmo drew him onward until they stood in front of the silent figures. They stared at them unbelievingly. Sightless eyes stared back at them.

'But what —? How —?' Cosmo dropped Pesky's arm and circled the figures, moving down the row of seats behind them. He stopped abruptly.

'What is it?' Connie called out. 'What happened to them?'

'Knives . . .' Cosmo put out his hand and drew it back. 'Stilettos . . . They — They've been *skewered* to their seats — right through the back of their chairs!'

CHAPTER 7

Empress Josephine?' Dr Parker snorted. 'They ought to call this floating charnel house the *Madame Defarge!*'

'That isn't funny!' Carl Daniels glared at Parker. He'd been on duty for hours, accepting the large envelopes filled with jewellery and returning them to the safe-deposit boxes lining the back wall of the Purser's Office. Lulled by the fact that nothing dire had happened all day, he had begun to hope that the death threat had been a hoax. And now this.

'It wasn't meant to be.' Parker was calm — perhaps too calm. The bodies were laid out in sick bay. Laid out was not quite the right description. In the air-conditioned chill of the cinema, rigor mortis had begun and the bodies were locked in a sitting position. No one had wanted to break bones in order to straighten them out into the conventional position. In the end, the entire front row of nine seats had been unbolted and conveyed to the hospital with its grim cargo intact.

'Sorry. Point taken.' More than one point, perhaps. Daniels lowered his eyelids, partly in weariness, partly so that a newly-formed suspicion shouldn't be shown. Five dead bodies, each neatly skewered from behind through the heart. And without striking a bone. Surely that betrayed some medical knowledge.

Furthermore, the method of murder suggested an inside knowledge of minutiæ of shipboard life. Those cinema seats were new. The old moulded plastic ones had been replaced during the recent refit. None of the passengers would be likely to realize that the new seats were of woven plastic, padded with foam rubber, and then covered by the usual red plush. Easily penetrated, as events had proved.

How much did they know about Dr Jack Parker? His credentials had obviously been good enough to secure the job — for whatever that was worth. Did the Line take up references? Or were they too pleased to get a reasonably young and personable doctor to inquire too deeply into his past and the reasons he might be willing to immure himself in a dead end job?

The reason he had given was par for the course: he had been seriously ill and wished to spend a few years in a not-too-arduous job while he recovered his health and strength. 'Seriously ill' could cover anything from acute alcoholism to a complete psychiatric breakdown. What was it in Parker's case? It was time to take a look into his background — and perhaps a few other backgrounds — and try to find out what certain people might be trying to hide.

Joan was groggy with fatigue. She had been helping Carl in the Purser's Office. They had just closed up when he had been called away to deal with the latest crisis.

She didn't want to think about that just now. It was enough that none of the crew had been involved, despite their forebodings. All she wanted right now was to fall into bed and sleep for a week. Or at least until morning when she might be strong enough to face the world again.

A wavering uncertain figure appeared at the end of the

passageway and advanced, hesitantly at first, then with growing purposefulness as she saw Joan's uniform. Instinctively Joan knew that she didn't want to hear what was about to be said. She looked about, but there was no escape; it was too late to turn around and go back the way she had come. They were on a collision course.

'Oh, stewardess, perhaps you could help me.' The passenger hailed her anxiously. 'I've looked everywhere for my friend and I can't find her. I don't know what to do next.'

'Oh?' Joan tried not to look too concerned while her heart sank. 'When did you —?'

'I'm Miss O'Fallon, from B Deck. I share a cabin with my friend, Miss O'Rierdon. We're school teachers — that is, we were. We've just retired and we thought we'd take a cruise to celebrate. And we've been enjoying it very much. I suppose it's silly of me to worry, but Miss O'Rierdon hasn't come back to the cabin and it *is* quite late.'

'She might have met friends,' Joan suggested mechanically. 'If she's not in any of the bars, she might have gone back to their cabin with them for a nightcap.'

'*Not* at this hour!' Miss O'Fallon was shocked. 'Why, it's nearly two o'clock in the morning!'

'Is it really?' Joan had lost all track of time.

'That's why I'm worried,' Miss O'Fallon said. 'I'm trying not to be silly, but it's so awfully late and she's never done anything like this before. I've been sitting down in the cabin thinking perhaps she decided to take a turn around the deck after the movie. The deck is so wet and slippery, I'm afraid she might have fallen overboard.'

'No,' Joan said faintly. 'I can assure you that no one has fallen overboard.'

'Then where is she?'

It was inevitable. Most people on holiday travelled in pairs. Had any of the other victims had companions who were now out looking for them?

'You say she went to the cinema?' Joan played for time.

'That's right. I didn't go because I'd already seen the film on shore. It wasn't so good I wanted to sit through it again.'

And that may just have saved your life. Perhaps something of what she was thinking was mirrored in her eyes. Miss O'Fallon suddenly looked frightened.

'What did you say your friend's name was — is?' Joan tried to look as though she had just remembered something.

'O'Rierdon. Maureen O'Rierdon.'

'Ah yes —' Joan averted her eyes from the hopeful gaze and, for the good of the ship, tried to lie convincingly. 'I do believe someone from B Deck reported to the Doctor's Office after the cinema. She wasn't feeling well and Dr Parker put her into sick bay overnight. In case she was coming down with something infectious. I'm almost sure the name was O'Something. Shall I check and find out if it's your friend?'

'Oh, would you? Or perhaps I ought to go along myself and see how she is . . .' The woman frowned and hesitated. The magic word 'infectious' had done its work.

'You wouldn't be able to see her. She'll be sleeping now and you wouldn't want to disturb her. I'm sorry no one let you know where she was.'

'Oh, I understand,' Miss O'Fallon said. 'These things can happen. It's probably Maureen's fault. She can be awfully vague at times.'

'Why don't you go back to your cabin and get some rest? I'll check on your friend and telephone you — but I'm almost certain she's in sick bay.'

'Oh, thank you,' Miss O'Fallon said. 'If she's awake, tell her I'll visit her in the morning.'

'Why don't you sleep late and not worry about that?' Joan suggested quickly. 'Your stewardess will bring you breakfast in your cabin. Late morning — or afternoon — would be better for visiting, anyway.'

'That's a good idea. I've lost a lot of sleep tonight, but now that I know my friend is all right . . .'

Carl Daniels cursed vehemently as Joan reported the incident. 'I don't see how we can keep the lid on this much longer.'

'Perhaps we're not supposed to,' Dr Parker said. 'Those last murders were done in a pretty public place. It was just luck — and the fact that they were all sitting in the front row — that no one noticed when the audience filed out. But people don't think anything of it if some remain seated until the rush for the exits thins out a bit.'

'The projectionist should have noticed!' Captain Falcon spoke between clenched teeth. Another flaming fool who kept his eyes shut — or as good as. They had expected the next victims to be crew members — and the crew knew it. Working alone, the projectionist had barricaded himself in his booth and fled towards bright lights and company as soon as the film had ended. He had turned off the lights without checking the auditorium — and without noticing five people slumped in their seats down front.

'I tell you one thing —' Jacques was looking pale and faintly green, he had just viewed the bodies. 'Those knives they are killed with. They are not the same as the knife Edgar carries. They are not like any knives in my dining-room or kitchen. They have been brought on board especially!'

'That's a starting-point,' Daniels said. 'If the killer brought knives aboard, who knows what other deadly weapons he might have carried in his luggage.'

'Search the ship!' Captain Falcon commanded. 'If anyone complains, we'll throw them in the brig! Most of them ought to be in there, anyway.'

'It needn't come to that,' Daniels said. 'The cabin staff will be able to make an inconspicuous search in the course of their duties. For the rest of the ship, we'll announce that we're having a fire drill for crew only — passengers know that's standard on every voyage — then we'll carry out the bomb search procedure. That ought to turn up anything there is to find.' There had not yet been a bomb threat against the *Empress Josephine* — yet — but, in common with most other ships, she was prepared for the eventuality. Her crew ran periodic bomb drills searching for a hidden device, carefully planted in a different location each time. They had always located the 'bomb' in less than fifteen minutes.

'The idea of an infectious disease is a good one, Joan,' Dr Parker said. 'I think we ought to ride with that for a while. It will explain the missing passengers — and make sure that no one wants to visit them.'

'I don't like it,' Captain Falcon said. 'I don't want my ship to get a reputation as a plague ship.'

'Would you rather the passengers knew the truth?'

'We have no real choice,' Daniels pointed out. 'The passengers will be able to cope with the idea of a mystery virus going the rounds. There'd be panic if they realized there was a maniac on board striking down people at random.'

'But *why*?' Joan looked at the grim faces. 'Why should anyone do these terrible things? You call him a maniac, but if he brought weapons aboard with him, that means he planned it all. I could believe in someone suddenly going berserk once on board, but I find it harder to believe in premeditated madness.'

'Another good point, Joan.' Parker nodded. 'Perhaps we ought to start looking for a link between the victims. Someone might be paying off old scores.'

'Me — I can believe in premeditated madness!' Jacques's eyes blazed — for a moment he looked mad himself. 'I am old enough to have seen it inflame a Continent. Look to the German, that is what I say! He, too, is the right age. It would be interesting to know what position he held in the Third Reich. Perhaps —' he stretched his lips mirthlessly — 'perhaps he is an old Concentration Camp Commandant who has reverted to the days of his youth — when killing people was so much a part of the day's work.'

'Now that's enough!' Captain Falcon spoke loudly, but without heat. No possibility could be considered too far-fetched at this point. 'We'll look into it,' he promised. 'As soon as it's daylight, we'll start Head Office checking through everybody's backgrounds. They won't like it, but they'll have to do it.' His mouth tightened grimly.

'It's the only help they can be to us. Other than that, we're on our own.'

'*It's three o'clock in the morning* . . .' D-and-D hummed to himself as he strolled down the deserted passageway. Of course, it might only be two o'clock, or possibly four, or five. Somewhere along the way, he seemed to have lost track of time. Not that it mattered. Nowhere to go and nothing to do on this ship. Bars all closed, gambling casino shut, lights dimmed everywhere. He was probably the only one on the whole ship who was still awake.

'*Just one more waltz* . . .' he hummed encouragingly. '*Just one more drink . . . with you* . . .' With anyone. Where had all the people gone? It couldn't be that late. Night was young. Just starting. Must be. How else did he feel so refreshed and invigorated?

Of course, maybe he had had a nice little nap somewhere. Not his cabin, no. He'd have remembered leaving it. As it was, he had only a vague recollection of struggling to his feet from the depths of something soft and squishy and starting off on his wandering again. Nothing unusual about that.

The Flying Dutchman, that was him. Condemned to wander without rest until he found . . . until he found . . . the sixth bar! That was the answer. A nice little nightcap in the sixth bar and he could rest in peace. But where was it?

Maybe it was a ghost bar, appeared only during midnight hours, vanishing with the first ray of dawn. In that case, this was the right time to look for it.

Time? He brought his wristwatch up to within six inches of his eyes, but the hands wavered mockingly, the numbers refused to materialize for him. The witching hours, anyway. Definitely the witching hours.

He reached the end of the corridor suddenly, still concentrating on his watch, and stumbled into the lobby. Dark though it was, it seemed to vibrate with a sense of movement, as though people had just walked through it.

He blinked around. The locked latticework grille of the Purser's Office gleamed dully, the doors to the Radio Room and the Doctor's Office were closed. Maybe they had just shut down for the night. Maybe the officers were just ahead of him and, if he hurried, he could catch up with them and they could all go and have a nice drink. Maybe they were even heading for the sixth bar.

D-and-D hurried forward eagerly. Surely there was someone just down that corridor —? No. Maybe the next one —? No. Or, not quite. They must have gone up the stairs. D-and-D gripped the railing and began to hoist himself up.

Someone just ahead was whistling faintly, an old sea shanty he hadn't heard for years. He reached the top of the stairs and looked around. No one in sight. The whistle still echoed and he took up the refrain. Perhaps, if the whistler heard it, he'd know someone else was awake and wait for him to catch up. How did it go? Oh yes . . .

'*Wrap me up in my tarpaulin jacket* . . .' D-and-D carolled heartily. '*Dum-dum-de-do* . . .

> '*Wrap me up in my tarpaulin jacket* . . .
> '*Here comes a poor sinner below* . . .'

He was grabbed from behind and slammed against the wall. Shaken and slammed again, his head bouncing off the wall. Instinctively, he began to fight back, trying to figure out what was happening to him.

'I've got him!' Some nut in a jogging suit was screaming. 'I've got the bastard!' The nut kept playing rat-a-tat-tat on the wall with his head. Not content with that, hands began clawing for his throat.

'Wait a minute —' D-and-D gurgled. 'I can explain —' He wasn't sure what he had to explain, but he must have done something.

'Pesky — cut it out!' Another nut in a jogging suit joined the first, but he seemed to be on D-and-D's side. He was trying to pull the other one away.

'Pesky — what's the matter?' Cosmo prised the hands away from D-and-D's throat just as he was beginning to turn a nasty shade of crimson. 'Take it easy, Pesky. Don't crack up now!'

'Easy?' Pesky snarled. 'Easy? Didn't you hear him? I've got him. I've caught the maniac!'

'Maniac, yourself, ol' boy.' D-and-D rubbed his aching throat and appealed to his rescuer. 'I was just walking along, minding m'own business 'n' this madman leaped on me and began trying to kill me! Got a good mind to report him to the Captain. Nut like that shouldn't be left running around loose.' D-and-D had been shocked almost into sobriety.

'I'm terribly sorry, Mr Smithers. I can't imagine what got into him —' Cosmo turned to Pesky. 'What *did* get into you?'

'I heard him,' Pesky said wildly. 'Didn't you hear him? You were right behind me. He was singing —'

'Law 'gainst that now, is there?' Now that the shock was over, things were beginning to get misty again. Not helped by nonsense being babbled. 'What if I was?'

'I didn't hear anything, Pesky.' Cosmo frowned anxiously. 'Look, you've had a bad few days. Why don't you go back to bed? I'll take the joggers round by myself.'

'He was singing —' Pesky paused for emphasis. 'He was singing *Wrap Me Up In My Tarpaulin Jacket*!'

'He was?' Cosmo was jarred.

'No law 'gainst that. 'F there is, why don't you go and get the other guy? He was whistling it first. Never would've thought of it, otherwise. Haven't heard it in years.'

'What other guy?' Pesky advanced menacingly. D-and-D shrank back. 'What are you talking about?'

'Someone jus' ahead. Leading me to the sixth bar. *He* started whistling it first. Get him, why don't you?'

'What other guy? Where? Who?'

'Don' know, ol' man.' D-and-D blinked at Pesky owlishly.
'Wasn't you, was it?'

CHAPTER 8

The white envelope was waiting on the counter, thrust well back
from the grille, when Daniels opened the office in the morning.
He read it and immediately went to the Captain with it.

On the fifth day out, five died.
On the sixth day out, six will die.
On the seventh day, seven.
And so it must go on . . .
Unless . . .

'Unless?' Captain Falcon turned the page. 'Unless what?'
This time there were instructions — insolent, impossible instructions. Captain Falcon read them, growing increasingly
apoplectic.

'I won't do it!' he bellowed. 'The passengers won't do it! This
is extortion!'

'It's demanding money with menaces,' Daniels said. 'Holding an entire ship to ransom.' Curiously, he felt happier than he
had for days. It was out in the open now — and there was a
reason behind the killings. They were not the work of a madman
striking at random, but the coldly calculated plan of a vicious
killer, designed as a softening-up process to prepare the Captain
and officers of the *Empress Josephine* for the demand which had
just arrived.

'At least we know what we're dealing with now.' Daniels even
smiled. 'I'd rather deal with a thief than a maniac.'

'Don't get too happy about it,' Dr Parker warned. 'Just
because there's a method in his madness, it doesn't mean that
he's any the less mad.'

'I won't deal with this murderer — maniac or not!' Captain Falcon thundered. 'Apart from anything else, what he wants isn't ours to give. We can't turn the contents of the safe-deposit boxes over to him. They belong to the passengers.

'Why, why — God damn it!' Full realization had just come to Captain Falcon. 'This is piracy!'

'Piracy — modern style,' Daniels agreed. He had had longer to consider the matter than the others. 'We know it happens in the South China Sea. We know the Caribbean has become notorious for it — they estimate 1500 victims have died there. Cabin cruisers and yachts are hi-jacked, their owners and crews slaughtered; then the boats are used for a drug-smuggling run or two and scuttled before the Coast Guard has time to realize they're missing. I suppose it was only a matter of time before they began targeting luxury liners and using more sophisticated methods. We've been boarded by a pirate carrying a ticket, as a fare-paying passenger —'

'Or possibly —' Dr Parker interjected quietly — 'one of the crew.'

'If I thought that,' Captain Falcon said, 'I'd throw every man jack of them in irons!'

'Boarded — or infiltrated —' Daniels was still thinking it through. 'Instead of passengers being forced to walk the plank, as in the old days, they're quietly being slaughtered and left for us to put over the side.'

'And more of them every day,' Captain Falcon said grimly. '*Unless* . . . Unless! God damn it! — the old-fashioned pirates were more honest. They walked among the passengers themselves with a collecting basket for them to throw their valuables into. This son of a sea-cook expects us to do it for him!'

'Not easy,' Daniels agreed. 'Especially since the passengers don't know anything about the situation. The way we've managed to keep the lid on it must be very frustrating for him.' No wonder the last set of killings had been in such a public place — and how doubly frustrating to the pirate that they had passed unnoticed.

Possibly doubly dangerous. Would he now be driven to wilder excesses to bring the situation to the attention of the passengers? It was more than possible, it was highly probable. The passengers would not give up their valuables without good reason. A short sharp lesson emphasizing their vulnerability was in order. But what?

'The search has started?' Captain Falcon asked. 'The cabin staff know what they're looking for?'

'Anything that could be used as a weapon,' Daniels confirmed. 'If they can recognize it. Those stilettos were probably the most blatant part of the arsenal he brought on board. If we could have found them before he'd used them, we'd have had him dead to rights. As it is . . .'

'He's used something different each time, that isn't going to make it any easier. Do you think —?' Dr Parker glanced from the Captain to the Purser uneasily. 'I was wondering . . . the idea about infection. Joan hit on it, but it's fairly obvious. And it would kill or incapacitate a lot of people at one stroke. I was wondering if it might not be a good idea to turn off the air-conditioning system. It's the first thing we're supposed to do in case of fire because of the danger of pumping smoke and fumes into all the cabins. If he were to put something into the system . . .'

'It's an idea,' Daniels said reluctantly. 'It was the air-conditioning system that spread Legionnaire's Disease in those hotels, wasn't it? The fact was well publicized and it's a good guess that our pirate would have read about it. The question is, would he have access to dangerous germs?'

A doctor would be able to acquire germs — or manufacture them. Again, Daniels felt the mistrust of Parker. It could be a double bluff on his part. Warning them of the next step in the campaign under the guise of being helpful.

'Turn off the air-conditioning?' Captain Falcon asked incredulously. 'With this ship sailing through the tropics? This is supposed to be a luxury cruise — not a foretaste of hell!'

'It's working up to a pretty good foretaste right now,' Parker said. 'It will be your responsibility if you don't turn off the air-conditioning and the system is used to disseminate germs.'

'It's my responsibility, anyway, mister!' Captain Falcon snapped.

'I think it's a risk,' Daniels agreed, 'but I don't think it's an immediate danger. Later he might try something wholesale like that. Today he's only threatened to kill six. I'm sorry —' he choked as he realized what he'd just said. 'I didn't mean *only* —'

'We know what you mean,' Captain Falcon said grimly. 'It's understandable, given the circumstances. There's one thing I can do, though, and I'm going to do it. I've never been a man to run from a fight, but I can admit it when it's the only sensible thing to do. So, he's going to kill us off at an increasing rate each day, is he? Well, I'm going to cut the days out from under him.

'Gentlemen, this ship is going to tuck her tail between her legs like a kicked cur and race for port!'

Who would have imagined that Mrs Anson-Pryce carried a gun around with her?

It was a very pretty gun — beautiful, even. But, Mrs Anson-Pryce? Joan stared down at it unbelievingly.

It lay in a nest of pastel lingerie, looking right at home on top of the silk and lace. It was pearl-handled and the elegantly chased barrel might have been silver-plated, or perhaps genuine platinum. But there was no doubt at all that it could do the required amount of damage to anyone who got in its way. In Mrs Anson-Pryce's way.

It reminded Joan of a fact they had all discounted earlier: Mrs Anson-Pryce had been one of the skeet-shooting party on the fatal day.

Staring down into the drawer, bemused, she did not hear the click of the latch behind her. Footsteps made no sound across the carpeted floor.

'Aaa-hem!' The sudden throat-clearing sound came from immediately behind her.

Joan leaped, trying to replace the top layers of lingerie and close the drawer at the same time. There was no mistaking those vocal chords — or the disapproval they were registering.

'I'm not disturbing you, I hope,' Mrs Anson-Pryce cooed in deceptively dulcet tones. 'I keep a personal diary, but I'm afraid it's locked in one of my cases in the hold. Perhaps you'd like to borrow my keys and slip down and read it? I'm *so* sorry I don't have it up here with me — but I didn't think there'd be anything worth recording happening on the voyage.'

'I — I —' Joan stammered. 'I was just —'

'I can *see* what you were doing!' Mrs Anson-Pryce's gaze lingered on the frill of lace trapped outside the drawer. She sniffed sharply. 'I suppose you've been drinking again!'

Joan tried to hold her breath and not exhale, thus confirming Mrs Anson-Pryce's worst suspicions. With what they knew, it was a wonder the entire crew didn't go reeling through their days. Except that they didn't dare — in case the killer caught them off guard.

'I thought as much! This is insupportable. After I warned you! This time I *will* report you to the captain.'

'Yes, ma'am,' Joan said. 'Just as you like, but it won't make any difference. The captain understands. There are . . . extenuating circumstances.'

'Oh?' Mrs Anson-Pryce was diverted, scenting drama — perhaps scandal. 'Are there? It's a broken heart, I suppose. That's usually the excuse. It's not worth it, my girl, take my word for it. Pull yourself together and forget him.'

'I will,' Joan pledged. 'I just need a bit more time. It's — it's so recent.' She was throwing herself into the character Mrs Anson-Pryce had thrust upon her. It seemed safer that way. Not only was it necessary to stop Mrs Anson-Pryce from bothering Captain Falcon but, if she *did* have anything to do with the series of killings, it would be safer to pretend to be the fool the older woman thought her.

'Recent, is it?' Mrs Anson-Pryce's eyes gleamed with interest.

'Yes.' Unbidden, the image of Waring rose before her. There hadn't been anything between them — well, not very much —

but she had been fond of him. There might have been, except that she preferred Carl Daniels. Poor Waring. She felt tears form and was aware that Mrs Anson-Pryce was looking almost sympathetic.

'He died —' Joan allowed the might-have-been full sway. Poor, poor Waring. 'Very suddenly.' Her voice quavered. 'Just before the ship sailed.'

'Pesky's cracking up.' Cosmo voiced his fears to Connie. 'Understandable, of course, but it won't make him any the more reliable on stage.'

'Especially as he hasn't had a minute to study his lines,' Connie agreed.

'That, too,' Cosmo grinned. 'So I told him to forget about the matinee and take it easy. We'll switch to *Red Peppers* — we should have stuck to it, anyway.'

'Thank goodness we brought the costumes.' Connie gave a final twitch to the tunic of her sailor suit and reached for the red wig. Cosmo's red wig was already in place, making him look odd and unfamiliar. 'What about the music?'

'Mel's got it. He's out there now —' The piano outside began tinkling a selection of Noel Coward songs. The audience rustled expectantly.

'You see? No problem. He was glad to do it. It gives him a chance to pull out from the rest of the group and do something on his own.' Cosmo smiled triumphantly, becoming familiar again — and impossibly dear to her.

'Best of all, no one will complain about the programme switch. We've got a captive audience out there —' His smile faded. 'I wish I hadn't said that!'

'Oh, Cosmo!' She dropped the wig on to the dressing-table and hurled herself into his arms. 'Cosmo, I'm so scared. I'm scared of dying. I'm even more scared of your dying and leaving me behind alone!'

'Hey — that's not going to happen!' His arms tightened around her. 'Tell you what we'll do. To hell with our schedules!

We'll stick together. We won't be separated for a minute. We'll stick so close, he'll be able to get both of us with one shot. If we go, we'll go together.'

'Oh, Cosmo . . . thanks!' The piano music was becoming more urgent, leading up to their cue. She snatched up her red wig and fitted it on hurriedly.

'Hurry up —' Cosmo reached out and tugged at the wig, giving it a rakish tilt. 'We're on!'

They caught up the prop telescopes, linked arms, matched steps and danced onstage to the tune of a sailor's hornpipe, singing:

'Has anybody seen our ship . . . ?'

One by one the crew search parties reported back — with nothing to report. The cabin staff had more to report, interesting details, but not necessarily incriminating.

Nevertheless, Daniels made a note of them, as he had noted the names of the skeet-shooters. There were a lot of them but, somewhere, enough lines must intersect to point in a definite direction. If only they had more information. There was no way of pinpointing those who had been near by when the victims of the first three days had been despatched.

It had taken them so long to realize that those deaths had been deliberate. Perhaps they would not have realized it yet, if it had not been for the first letter. Why had it taken the killer so long to come out into the open? Was it because they had been so slow in recognizing his work? Or was there another reason?

He hadn't claimed responsibility until the end of the fourth day out. He must have known that he might not be believed immediately. The Captain had to consider the possibility that some oddball had stumbled over the victims of the accidental shootings and decided to bolster whatever passed as his ego by pretending that he had been responsible. In many cases on shore the police were hampered by a regular quota of nuts who rushed forward to confess. And the *Empress Josephine* carried her fair share of nuts on every voyage.

The pirate had known that it would take another set of killings to convince the ship's authorities that he was in earnest. So, late on the evening of the fifth day, he had killed again and the bodies had not been discovered until well after midnight. He could not have known that they would be discovered so soon. According to his calculations, he must have expected them to be found when they opened the cinema the next morning.

If he was calculating the timing that closely, there must be a reason: by the end of the fifth day, the *Empress Josephine* had passed her point of no return. It would be faster for her to continue on course to Nhumbala than to return to Miami.

That meant there were accomplices on shore in Nhumbala, person or persons who had arranged for the pirate to get ashore safely with his booty. How else could he walk off the ship and through Nhumbalan Customs carrying the jewellery and money he planned to take from the passengers? Bribes might even now be changing hands in port.

Or perhaps a yacht had been hi-jacked to rendezvous with the *Empress Josephine* and pick up the pirate. It wouldn't take much to keep everyone at bay while he transferred to the smaller boat — one hostage would do.

The problem in demanding ransom was always that of collecting it and getting away safely with it. On shore. But a light yacht could go into channels too shallow for the cruise liner. The pirate could sail away laughing, knowing the *Empress Josephine* dare not risk ripping her hull open by pursuing him.

When? Daniels stared at the grim column of mathematics marching down the page. Fifteen people had died to date. The pirate had threatened six more deaths today, which would bring the total to twenty-one. If he continued killing progressively, as he had also threatened, by the end of the voyage — on the tenth day — fifty-five people would have been killed. Slaughtered. Provided the ransom hadn't been paid.

Even if the ransom were paid, could the killer afford to stop there? He must know that, once he had shown himself as he abandoned ship, he would leave hundreds of witnesses who could identify him later.

He was a ruthless callous killer; he had proved that abundantly. Would he consider a few hundred more lives well lost to ensure his future safety? Would he just board a boat and chance being able to slip into another identity with the help of the ransom and possibly plastic surgery? Or would the vessel collecting him be a gunboat which would turn those guns on the *Empress Josephine* and sink her as it sailed away?

In the Radio Room next door, Sparks was frowning over his set. He was trying to get through to Head Office to relay their urgent request for information and help, but he was having trouble.

The Shipping Office in Nhumbala was jamming the air waves to Head Office and, alternately, to the *Empress Josephine*, but the messages were almost impossibly garbled. It was only possible to decipher that no good was being broadcast.

Sparks adjusted various instruments, cursing under his breath, and tried to make sense of the messages.

CHAPTER 9

Stealthily the *Empress Josephine* picked up speed — as though she could outdistance the thing she carried in her.

Carl Daniels was conscious of it as he frowned at the notes he had made. She was a good ship; if she tried hard enough, she might cut thirty-six hours or more off their schedule — and she was trying.

'Excuse me —' Timid but determined, the voice spoke from the doorway. 'You *are* the Purser, aren't you?'

'Yes, ma'am.' Carl rose quickly, advancing to meet her before she could come into the office and perhaps glimpse the notes. 'Can I help you?'

'I'm Miss O'Fallon,' she said. 'From B Deck. I've just been to the hospital, but the door is locked and no one seems to be around. I want to visit my cabinmate — she's in there.'

'Oh, uh —' He was momentarily taken aback. *Where was Parker? It was up to him to deal with this situation.* 'Just a minute, Miss O'Fallon. I'll be right with you.'

He gathered up his papers and took them into the back office where he locked them in a desk drawer. Then he lifted the telephone and dialled the Doctor's Office. There was no answer. Reluctantly he returned to the outer office.

'I was distinctly told,' Miss O'Fallon said, 'that I could see my friend this afternoon. There's nothing worse than being sick in strange surroundings. I've brought the book she was reading and some magazines and I'll sit with her for a while and cheer her up.'

'She may be sleeping —'

'Then I can sit there and wait until she wakes.' Miss O'Fallon's voice was rising. Passengers crossing the lobby were glancing curiously towards the latticework grille. 'I have nothing else to do.'

'All right.' At least, he could get her out of public view. 'We'll go along to the hospital and see.'

'It was locked a few minutes ago.' Mollified, she trotted along beside him, clutching her tote bag of reading materials. 'That's why I came to you. I thought you might have a key.'

'We'll have to find the doctor first —' Carl sidestepped the implied question. 'He has the final say as to whether or not your friend should receive visitors.'

'I'll just pop in for a minute, then,' she said earnestly. 'I won't try to stay, if he doesn't think I should. But poor Maureen will feel so lonely and neglected if no one goes near her.'

'You're a very kind woman. Not many people would be willing to risk . . .' He hesitated. 'Risk serious infection.'

'Oh!' She stopped short, eyes widening with consternation. 'Then it *is* serious?'

'I'm afraid so.' As serious as it could get, but he could not admit that yet. 'The doctor is still running tests.'

'But . . . how could she have caught anything here on board?'

'That's it,' he improvised quickly. 'She must have caught it ashore and brought it on board with her. The doctor said the incubation period is just about right.'

'But . . .' Miss O'Fallon was bewildered. 'In that case, what about me? I've been with her all along, sharing the same cabin. Shouldn't I be in the hospital, too?'

It was a good question; one he should have foreseen. Miss O'Fallon moved towards the hospital door, as though ready to go in and lie down. Daniels hoped the door was still locked.

Fortunately, it was. All they needed was for Miss O'Fallon to swing open the door on a row of empty beds and the fat would be in the fire.

'You see —' She pushed against the unyielding door. 'No one can get in to see even the doctor, let alone the patients. Shouldn't someone be on duty in there?'

'Yes, I think you ought to see the doctor as soon as possible.' She had given him an idea. 'I mean, you look rather . . . Are you sure you're feeling quite all right?'

'Well . . . I . . .' She released the doorknob, her hand fluttered to her forehead. 'I . . . *do* feel a bit feverish . . . dizzy . . . I thought I might be getting seasick. The ship *does* seem to be rolling more than usual today.'

'Perhaps you ought to go back to your cabin and lie down,' Daniels suggested. 'I'll find Dr Parker and send him to you.'

'Yes . . . thank you. Perhaps that would be best . . .' She turned away and just missed colliding with D-and-D who had come loping down the corridor.

'Whoa, there —' He caught at her, steadying himself. 'No hurry. Nowhere to go onna ship. Come'n have a drink with me.'

'*No*, thank you.' Miss O'Fallon drew herself up, offended.

'Aw, c'mon. We'll find a nice quiet bar. Sixth musht be quiet — nobody can ever find it. But we will.'

'*No!*' She shook off his hands and retreated hastily.

'Mos' unfriendly ship I've ever been on.' D-and-D blinked

muzzily after her. 'How about you, ol' boy? Join me in a drink?'

'Sorry, I'm on duty.' Glancing beyond the passenger, Daniels saw Pesky Calhoun's head appear round the corner. Pesky pantomimed for secrecy and disappeared again.

'Mos' unfren'ly ship . . .' D-and-D sighed and moved on.

Daniels waited while Pesky reappeared and approached silently, keeping close to the wall, keeping his eyes fixed on D-and-D.

'Shhh!' The warning was unnecessary. Daniels was speechless anyway. He managed to raise an inquiring eyebrow.

'It's him!' Pesky hissed as he drew abreast. 'He's the one who's doing it! He's the killer!'

'Him?' Daniels regained his voice. 'He couldn't kill anything except a bottle of bourbon.'

'Don't you believe it! That's what we're meant to think. But I caught him —'

'What? You caught him killing —?'

'Er, not exactly.' Pesky looked a bit shamefaced. 'I caught him whistling —'

Daniels began to laugh.

'No, listen — it's serious. I caught him singing *Wrap Me Up In My Tarpaulin Jacket.*'

Daniels stopped laughing abruptly.

'You see? Why would he be singing that if he didn't *know*? And how could he know if he wasn't doing it? We've kept it quiet enough. Oh no. He was *taunting* us!'

'Him?' Daniels watched D-and-D turn a corner and weave out of sight. 'That — that *lush?*'

'A pose — and a good one. He didn't drop it even when I — when I, er, challenged him.'

'What did he say?'

'He claimed somebody just ahead of him had been whistling it and he'd just picked up on the tune.'

'It could be true.' Daniels would find that easier to believe than that D-and-D was the brain behind the nightmare.

'I didn't see anybody ahead of him. Cosmo didn't, either.'

Pesky inched past Daniels, his burning eyes focused on the empty corridor. 'He's the one. I swear it!'

'Take it easy.' Daniels caught his arm, he was looking more wild-eyed by the moment. 'What are you going to do?'

'I'm going to tail him! I can't prove anything yet — but I'll tail him until I can. Then I'll —' Pesky's fists clenched.

'Then you'll bring him before the Captain! There's no other way, Pesky. Don't try it!'

'Yeah, sure,' Pesky agreed unconvincingly. 'That's what I meant.'

'Remember, he's a passenger. We've got to be very, very sure. We could be in big trouble, otherwise.'

'I'd say we were in big trouble now!' Pesky gave a short mirthless laugh and slipped out of Daniels's grip. 'Don't worry. I'm going to keep him in sight every minute. Then we'll all be safe. He won't dare do anything while I'm watching.'

Captain Falcon bared his teeth in what was meant to be an affable smile and took his place at the head of the table. 'Good evening, everyone,' he said.

'Good evening . . .' 'Good evening . . .' they answered him. The water quivered in the carafe in the centre of the table; the silverware shimmied together, jingling, and apart again with the movement of the ship.

'Say —' Mortimer Ordway caught a spoon as it slid away from his place setting. 'We seem to be moving along at a pretty good clip. We've picked up speed, haven't we?'

'I would not like to think so.' Herr von Schreiber frowned at the Captain. 'The faster a ship goes, the more fuel it uses. It would be wasteful to go too fast.'

'We are proceeding at our usual rate of knots.' Captain Falcon glanced from one to the other with distaste.

'Und also,' Frau von Schreiber said, 'if we go faster, we get there sooner. We have paid for ten days.'

'That's right,' Hallie Ordway put in. 'It wouldn't be fair to get less than we bargained for.'

Sometimes you get more than you bargain for. Captain Falcon transferred his look of dislike to the two women. 'This line has never short-changed anyone yet,' he snapped.

'Ach, good!' Herr von Schreiber beamed on him with unexpected approval. 'That is well said.'

Mrs Anson-Pryce moved her shoulders restlessly. It made little difference to her if the ship arrived a day early. On the whole, she thought she might prefer it. This was not a happy ship. Furthermore, she was losing heavily at bridge. Not that that would matter so much, if only she could have a decent game. But that woman, Madge, was a fool. She couldn't play a decent hand when she was dealt one and, what's worse, she didn't care. All she wanted to do was talk about her homes, her money, her jewellery, especially her diamonds.

Mrs Anson-Pryce smiled to herself and allowed her hand to go up to touch her diamond ear-rings, then fall lightly to her necklace. She had not intended to wear these on the crossing, they were too large and ostentatious. One couldn't wear them much anywhere, in fact; they were more of a portable treasury than adornments. But wait until that Madge set eyes on them tonight. That would put her in her place!

Behind her, she was aware that D-and-D's voice was rising insistently. That disgusting drunkard was creating another scene. How fortunate that he was not actually at her table, but how unfortunate that he was still so close.

'Ev'body join me inna drink!' he insisted. 'Waiter, we'll have a magnum of the — What's ev'ybody havin'? D'we want red or white?'

'No, really,' one of woman said. 'I don't want anything.' The others agreed with her. It was clear that what they would really like was a different table companion.

'Aw, c'mon. 'S a very good wine list —' He blinked at the dancing rows of print which refused to stay still and group themselves into words. 'Waiter —' he thrust the wine list back at him — 'you decide. Y'know what's travellin' well better'n I do. Red, I think. Red's always good.'

'I'm sorry,' one of the men said. 'I must decline to join you.' He added, on a note of inspiration, 'Doctor's orders, you know.'

'Yes, and my diet doesn't allow it,' one of the women chimed in quickly. 'I can only have water.'

'That's right,' someone else said. Suddenly the whole table were agreeing that they must only drink water.

'You can't drink that stuff,' D-and-D protested. 'Very bad for you. Can kill you, y'know. Rusts your guts —'

Mrs Anson-Pryce shuddered and tuned him out. Not that the conversation at her own table was any more scintillating.

'Say, I'm really looking forward to the Fancy Dress Ball tomorrow night.' Hallie Ordway leaned forward and twinkled at an unimpressionable Captain Falcon. 'Mortie and I have got the cutest costumes — just wait till you see them. They'll knock your eyes out. And —' she arched her eyebrows roguishly — 'I understand you're one of the judges.'

'Now, now, Hallie,' her husband said. 'You mustn't try to influence the judges.' He grinned around the table, in no doubt that Hallie could influence anyone she chose. 'It isn't fair to the others.'

Captain Falcon grunted noncommittally. If he had his way, the first prize would go to the first woman who came wearing no costume at all. He'd seen every other possible permutation of costume: cute, coy, pretty or grotesque. Pity that no woman would dare dispense with a costume altogether. He repressed a sigh, then brightened. One of them usually came as a harem dancer and that could be pretty good, depending on how flimsy the veils were.

Perhaps . . . he eyed Hallie speculatively, then dismissed the idea. No, too muscular. All those acrobatics. She might have the nerve and the lack of common sense to wear a harem outfit — but she wouldn't look all that good in it.

'Have you decided on your costume?' Hallie asked Mary Lawton.

'Oh, I don't know that I'll compete,' Mary said nervously. 'It isn't really my cup of tea.'

'I loathe costume balls,' Mrs Anson-Pryce pronounced. 'I *never* go in for that sort of thing.'

'Honey, you don't have to dress up any more than you do,' Hallie assured her. 'Those rocks put you in a class of your own. Just keep wearing them and you don't need any other outfit!'

He hadn't noticed. Captain Falcon blinked and looked at Mrs Anson-Pryce with new interest. She was, indeed, sporting an awesome array of gems. A queen's ransom — *or a ship's ransom*. He winced as the thought struck him, followed immediately by the vision of one of his officers holding a sack out in front of Mrs Anson-Pryce and waiting for her to strip off her gems and drop them into the sack. It was unthinkable! Surely the pirate must be aware of that. Mrs Anson-Pryce and passengers like her would not willingly give up their priceless treasures. It could not be done.

Mrs Anson-Pryce froze as all eyes centred on her — rudely. She lifted her head and stared beyond them — only to encounter another pair of eyes. Hostile eyes. So hostile they jarred her until she realized that they were not looking at her, but just behind her.

They were the eyes of that strangely named and most unsatisfactory Cruise Director, Pesky Calhoun.

She glared at him, even though he was too intent to notice. It was all his fault. She had been at an extremely amiable bridge table at first — until he had interfered. She had even won a small amount. That did not matter, however; it was the congenial company she had enjoyed. That nice funny little man who had been her partner and the charming sisters they had played against, the Misses Christopherson.

What had happened to them? Now that she thought about it, she had not seen any of them again. Surely all three of them could not have become seasick, but they seemed to have dropped out of all activities. Perhaps it was symptomatic of the malaise hanging over the entire ship.

'Mos' unfren'ly ship I've ever been on . . .' She heard D-and-D sigh behind her, as though in counterpoint to her own thoughts. The comment was punctuated by the gurgle of the wine bottle.

'Please pass the water.' Someone spoke pointedly.

'Y'know —' There was complimentary wine at the Captain's table and Hallie Ordway had been partaking generously. It was just what one might expect from that sort.

'Y'know —' Hallie leaned across the table, addressing Mrs Anson-Pryce earnestly. 'No kidding, honey. All you need to do is wear a green dress, hang all that stuff all over you — and you can go as a Christmas tree!'

'This mushroom soup is really very good —' Mary Lawton said quickly into the explosive silence that followed. 'I wish mine turned out so well. You must give my compliments to the chef, Captain.'

'If you tell the waiter,' Captain Falcon said stiffly, '*he'll* attend to that.' Did the idiot woman really imagine he was on terms like that with the chef?

'Oh dear,' Mary said softly, abruptly aware that she had committed a *faux pas* herself, while attempting to cover Hallie's.

'It *is* extremely tasty,' Mrs Anson-Pryce said graciously, prepared to forgive Mary and ignore Hallie. She glanced around at the soup plates; it seemed everyone had ordered it. 'And deservedly popular.'

'We had it that first night out.' Mary Lawton grasped the social straw gratefully. 'So I knew how good it was. I've been waiting for it to appear on the menu again.'

'*Soup, beautiful soup*,' D-and-D began chanting at the table behind, to the tune of *Mud, Glorious Mud* — he probably couldn't tell the difference. 'Ev'ybody loves mushroom soup . . .' his voice trailed off into a mutter. Undoubtedly under the quelling gaze of his unfortunate tablemates.

Mrs Anson-Pryce applied herself to her soup, but was unable to close her ears to the next amazing statement from the table behind her.

'That's better —' D-and-D said in a tone of pleased surprise. 'That's fren'lier. Jus' lay your head on my shoulder an' have a

THE CRUISE OF A DEATHTIME

li'l rest. Know jus' how you feel. Often feel that way myself.'

Mrs Anson-Pryce steeled herself not to turn around and look. She had seen the ladies on either side of D-and-D. Neither of them would be capable of such a breach of decorum had the man between them been a handsome film star, let alone a disgusting drunkard. He must have entered a further phase of his affliction and be hallucinating. He'd start talking about pink elephants next.

There was the sudden scrape of a chair being pushed back, then a crash as it overturned, followed by a dull thud. Choked voices cried out, there was a crash of dishes.

Mrs Anson-Pryce turned round just as a woman gave a gurgling scream and pitched face forward into her soup. And stayed there. The others at the table had either fallen to the floor or back against their chairs. There was, indeed, a woman slumped against D-and-D, her head resting on his shoulder. Of them all, D-and-D was the only one still upright. He continued to eat his mushroom soup with unconcern.

'What the devil —?' Captain Falcon began.

'EEEeeek!' Hallie Ordway rose to her feet with a blood-curdling scream. 'Look at them!' She pointed dramatically to the other table. 'Somebody *do* something! Get the doctor — quick! Can't you see? Those people are *dying!*'

Pandemonium swept the dining salon. People pushed back their chairs and stood for a better view. Several rushed forward. The waiters hastily set down trays and tried to restore order.

'Where's the doctor?' Captain Falcon thundered.

'Excuse me —' Carl Daniels said to his table. 'I'll go and see what the trouble is. Please remain seated. I'll be right back.' Even he knew how unlikely that was.

'It's him! It's him! I knew it!' Pesky Calhoun dashed across the room and pounced on D-and-D, yanking him to his feet. The woman who had been leaning against him slumped to the floor. She hit the edge of the table as she went down, knocking over his wine glass. Red wine spilled like blood across the crisp white tablecloth.

'What's happened?' Hallie screamed. 'What's the matter with them? Is it —?' She looked down at her plate in horror. 'Is it the mushroom soup?'

'It can't be,' Mrs Anson-Pryce said coldly. One more scream and she'd dash the jug of water in the creature's face. 'We've all eaten it and we're all right.' She was conscious of the faintest quiver in the pit of her stomach as she spoke. *Were* they all right? Had the other table been served first? If so . . .

'All right, steady as we go.' Captain Falcon took command. 'Get those people down to sick bay — fast! Put out a call on the tannoy for Dr Parker. Calhoun —' his voice rose above the uproar — 'put down that passenger!'

'But it's him! Don't you see? It's him!' Pesky was shaking D-and-D like a terrier with a rat. 'He isn't sick. That proves it! He's the only one at the table who's still all right.'

'He won't be, if you keep shaking him like that. Let go!' Daniels tore Pesky away from D-and-D, who sank back into his chair and stared muzzily around the table, as though wondering where everyone had gone. Absently he picked up his spoon and dipped it into this soup.

'Don't *do* that!' Captain Falcon knocked the spoon from his hand before it reached his lips. It clattered to the floor.

'Mos' unfren'ly ship I've ever been on —' D-and-D shook his head sadly. 'Fulla snobs and nut-cases.' He sighed deeply. 'Even th'Captain's a nut-case.'

'It's not the mushroom soup,' Pesky said suddenly, looking around. 'Other tables have eaten it and they'll all right. *He's* eaten most of his — and he's all right. It has to be something the rest of the table had and he didn't have —'

'The water —' Mrs Anson-Pryce said. 'The others refused to drink with him. I heard them. He offered them wine and they said they'd prefer water.'

'Water . . .' Carl Daniels looked down at the red stain on the tablecloth and the depleted water jug in the centre of the table. 'That could be it.'

'Mr Smithers —' He bent over and spoke slowly and distinctly. 'Mr Smithers, did you drink any of that water?'

'Drinka water?' D-and-D drew himself up with offended dignity. 'No, thank you, ol' boy. Never touch the stuff!'

CHAPTER 10

'How the bloody hell should I know what kind of poison it was?' Jack Parker's voice rose. 'I'm a doctor, not a toxicologist!'

'I just thought you might know.' Daniels was apologetic; everyone's nerves were frayed right now. 'Off the cuff, as it were.'

'Off the cuff, or on it —' Parker was heavily sarcastic — 'I *don't* know. There may not be any sure-fire unidentifiable mysterious South American or African poison that works instantaneously and leaves no trace, but there sure as hell are a few hundred so obscure that they can't be identified without a battery of laboratory tests — for which we are not equipped on this ship. Not to mention the new drugs the marvels of medical science keep throwing on to the market with side-effects yet to be discovered. A doctor is very lucky these days if he manages to cure the disease without killing the patient. I do not know the answer; I am unlikely to be able to find the answer. All I know is that I have five more cadavers who have been cut off in the prime of life. And —' He broke off, meeting Daniels's eyes.

'And the killer told us that six would die today,' Daniels finished for him. 'Smithers survived because he didn't drink the water. He may still be a target. I've sent him to his cabin and posted a guard outside the door —'

'I was going to say,' Parker cut in heavily, 'that it makes me furious. I am a medical man, sworn to nurture and protect life. The vicious, wanton waste I have witnessed since this voyage began makes me literally, physically sick! It must be stopped!'

'We'd welcome any practical suggestions,' Daniels said mildly. Parker's righteous indignation act was very effective. But there were still too many unanswered questions. Parker was a new boy aboard this vessel, still unproved. What was his background and why wasn't he in some sinecure ashore?

'Where were you earlier?' Daniels asked. 'You're supposed to be second sitting, but you weren't at your table. We had to put out a call for you.'

'It wouldn't have mattered if I had been there.' Parker was immediately on the defensive. 'Nothing could have saved them.'

'That doesn't answer my question!'

'It answers as much as you're entitled to ask.' Parker gave him a sardonic look. 'For the rest of it, let's just say that I was otherwise engaged. I was brought up to think of myself as a gentleman, so I won't mention her name.'

Joan? The force of rage that swept through him surprised Daniels. He had known he had a rival in Waring, but he had thought that the field was now clear.

'Gentlemen, please!' Captain Falcon called them to order. 'Personality conflicts are a luxury we cannot afford. We must concentrate on the common enemy.'

In the sudden silence, the knock at the door made them all jump. Then they realized that a killer would be unlikely to bother with such courtesies as knocking.

'Come in!' Captain Falcon bellowed.

'Dinner is served.' Jacques walked into the room, followed by Edgar, pushing a trolley of covered dishes. 'You did not get beyond the soup at dinner. You must eat and keep up your strength. You will be of no use if you cannot work and concentrate properly.'

'I ordered sandwiches and coffee,' Captain Falcon protested, with less fire than he might have shown.

'You need your proper meal.' As he spoke, Jacques expertly dealt napkins into laps, whisked lids off plates and set them before the correct individuals. It was clear that he had consulted the table waiters and knew what each officer had ordered just before bedlam had broken loose.

Edgar stood brooding behind the trolley, in no hurry to wheel it away once it had been depleted.

'Ah, well, you may be right,' Captain Falcon conceded, the sight of a medium-rare sirloin steak with Duchesse potatoes and green beans undermining his resolution. Sandwiches would not have been the same. 'You're a clever devil, Jacques.'

'Not I, but Napoleon,' Jacques demurred. 'Every army marches on its stomach. And, my friends, I think that we are an army right now, yes?'

'Yes.' They all spoke at once. Only Edgar abstained.

'And champagne —' Jacques lifted a bottle from the ice bucket, twirled a cloth around it and began worrying the cork with his thumbs — 'which goes with everything and yet leaves the clear head.' He sighed. 'We need the clear heads tonight.'

'Right again, Jacques,' Captain Falcon confirmed. He stabbed at his steak and watched the pink juice run into his plate. 'We've a stormy night ahead of us. We need all the energy we can muster.'

'You are all fools!' Edgar spoke out of turn, the flash of his eyes daring them to object. The influential blood relative who stood behind him almost visible in the shadows of his arrogance. 'What do you think you can do? You are powerless. Already this killer has proved that. You must delay no longer — you must send for help!'

'Help?' Captain Falcon put down his knife and fork and glared at Edgar. 'What help? Who the hell do you suggest we send for? We're a ship with a polyglot crew and a polyglot passenger list, registered under a flag of convenience, beyond any territorial waters . . . outside of any law. Who do you think we ought to send for: The CIA, the FBI, the SAS, the —'

The door burst open so quickly that no one could say whether there had been a perfunctory knock. The radio operator rushed into the room.

'Sir —!' He pulled himself up facing the Captain, not quite saluting. 'Sir, I've had a signal through from Head Office. There's civil war started in Nhumbala. The port is in rebel hands. Head Office says don't put into port there. Turn round and come straight back to Miami!'

They had locked him in his cabin and gone away and left him all alone.

Mos' unfren'lies' ship in the world . . . Never travel on thish line again . . .

D-and-D lurched across his cabin and found the flask he had providentially cached beneath his life-jacket in case of emergency and quaffed deeply. Thus refreshed, he returned to the door and hammered on it.

'Let me out,' he called, without any great confidence. 'I'm a payin' passenger. You can' do this to me!'

Silence answered him. He hadn't really expected anything else.

'Aw righ',' he said. 'Aw righ'.' He lowered himself to one knee and applied an eye to the keyhole.

Another eye stared back unblinkingly.

'Aw righ',' he muttered. But it was not all right with the other party.

'You just watch it, buddy —' The voice was so familiar it made his throat ache. 'I've got my eye on you. One false move and —'

D-and-D found himself jerking back and forth as though he were again being shaken, his head bouncing off the nearest vertical surface. Crazy . . . everybody on board this ship was crazy . . .

'Just watch it, that's all!' The eye disappeared and was replaced by a solid white substance. Somebody else — the crazy one was wearing evening clothes.

It was too much to cope with. D-and-D retreated to lie back on his bunk and take another long swallow from his flask. Never go this way again. Fly back . . . jet pilots weren't crazy — were they? Mus' be sanity somewhere inna world . . .

Never even got to finish his supper . . . only stupid mushroom

soup. Shut him away jus' because he wouldn't drink his water
. . . bad as school . . .

Hungry . . . awfully hungry. Time had passed and the gnawing in his stomach had intensified. His flask was empty . . . He
was lonely . . .

Hungry . . . didn' get enough to eat . . . never found the sixth
bar . . . Everybody against him . . .

He lurched to his feet, aided by a roll of the ship, and went
back to the door. Cautiously he peeked through the keyhole.
This time there was no one in view. Nothing except the opposite
wall of the corridor.

Cautiously, D-and-D tried the doorknob. It turned, but the
door was firmly locked.

Ah-ha-ha . . . they didn't get him that way! He was in a
double cabin, as he had noticed when he first walked in. That
meant there had been two keys — one for each presumed
occupant. They had taken away the one he kept in his pocket.
They didn't know he had squirrelled away the other key,
tucking it into the whistle pocket of his life-jacket; there had
been plenty of room for both the whistle and the key. No one
would ever think of looking for it there.

He dug it out, resisting the impulse to pipe a little tune on the
whistle. Quietly did it . . . don't draw any attention . . . don't
want an audience . . . jus' want freedom . . .

The key slid into the lock and turned noiselessly, the door
swung back. No one in front of the door . . . even a guard had to
go to the loo occasionally. No one to the left, no one to the right.
He darted into the corridor, closed the door silently behind him
and moved away swiftly.

He was free . . .

Cosmo was conducting the horse-racing in the main lounge.
Connie was sitting by his side turning the tumbler for the dice.
Since this was usually a job given to a favoured lady passenger,
there were some dark looks being cast in her direction and
mutterings about nepotism.

Connie didn't care. All that mattered was that Cosmo was keeping his promise and they were sticking together until death did them — She cut off the thought quickly. They were sticking together, that's all.

The Keep-Fit Class hadn't minded. In fact, they'd been most amused when Cosmo joined them earlier and solemnly went through their paces with them.

But that was this afternoon. The easily-started ripples of amusement had died away since the scene in the dining salon at dinner. The passengers were tense and upset, even though they had been assured that everything was all right. They didn't know the worst of it yet, but they were beginning to suspect that there was a lot more going on than they were being told. A rumour factory had sprung into spontaneous operation and more people were huddled together talking earnestly than were watching or betting on the horse-racing.

'Number Five advances four lengths,' Cosmo announced, reading the dice. The 'jockey' dutifully pushed her horse four squares ahead, it was now out in front of the field, but the usual excitement was lacking.

'Ooooh . . .' Hallie Ordway groaned. Her 'mount', Number Three, had been neck-and-neck in the lead with Number Five. Despite the fact that she had been so close to the stricken table, Hallie seemed to have regained her bounce. The brushing wings of the Dark Angel might have subdued the others, but not Hallie. Perhaps nothing could subdue the Ordways.

'Number Ten advances two lengths . . .' Cosmo continued calling. They were almost through the field of twelve runners and coming up to Hallie again. She was dancing impatiently beside her mount as though she could hardly wait. For once, Connie found the enthusiasm heartening; the others were being so withdrawn, just going through the motions while they thought about other things. Hallie had put everything out of her head except the game; she really *cared*.

'Number Three advances six lengths . . .'

'Wheee!' Hallie's squeal of delight drowned out all conversation in the lounge. She twisted round to look at her husband. 'We're winning, Mortie,' she shouted. 'We're winning!'

'We always do, babe!' he shouted back.

There was a spattering of applause. The Ordways were still everybody's favourite contestants.

'And it's Number Three in the lead and coming down the home stretch —' Cosmo picked up on the tentative animation, trying to whip it up into something like enthusiasm. The game had been dragging and this was the first sign of a spark.

'Yippee!' Hallie caught up her wooden horse and leapfrogged it from square to square. 'He's a steeplechaser and he's going to clear every hurdle and walk round the Winner's Circle with Momma!'

Connie twirled the dice tumbler with unnecessary force, hoping that Number Four or some other dark horse would unseat Hallie and romp home. Too bad it wasn't a genuine race with a sporting chance that she might break her neck or be trampled under hooves as she fell. Mortie, too, she amended her daydream as the male Ordway loosed something that was a cross between a Rebel yell and a Swiss yodel. No doubt about it, those two were beginning to grate on her nerves.

A sudden movement in the doorway drew her attention. D-and-D stood there, swaying. For a moment, it was familiar and natural, then she remembered with a shock that he was supposed to be locked in his cabin because he was under suspicion. Suspicion of what wasn't quite clear. One faction suspected him of being the killer, the other suspected that he was due to be the next victim.

Either way, he shouldn't be here. How had he got away from his guard? Shouldn't someone be told?

She turned to Cosmo but, when she turned back again, D-and-D had disappeared.

Joan hesitated at the door, reluctant to open it and step from the comparative safety of the crew's quarters into what she now thought of as the Front Line. Although some of the crew had been killed, it was becoming increasingly clear that the campaign of murder was aimed at the passengers. After all, they were the ones with the money and jewels to buy off the killer.

She glanced behind her, down the narrow utilitarian companionway, with bare pipes overhead and linoleum underfoot, dimly lit to save on electricity. All the behind-the-scenes cheeseparing of Victorian servants' quarters still existed on ships like this, unguessed at by the passengers — who would not have cared if they had guessed, so long as their own comfort was assured.

It was time to go on duty again, to turn down the beds in the luxury staterooms, to lay out pyjamas and nightdresses, to switch on reading lights so that people would not have to enter a dark room, to provide all the little touches of a first-class hotel.

She was the one who had to enter each dark cabin and bring it to glowing life. She did not want to. She was afraid of what she might find waiting.

The ship's bells chimed the hour. It was her watch. She could delay no longer. She turned the handle, edged the door ajar and stood listening for a moment. The adjacent passenger corridor seemed deserted. She stepped into it quickly, before her nerve could fail her, and closed the dividing door.

The lighting was subdued on this side, but not dim; the pipes were, for the most part, concealed behind panels; the carpeting was thick and luxurious underfoot.

She went to the Ordways' suite first; they usually left a light burning, sometimes two or three. She suspected they kept the lights on all day, whether they needed them or not. Nevertheless, it was comforting to walk into a lighted room tonight.

The next suite was less promising. It was strange how the von Schreibers had managed to turn the bright and spacious suite into something dark and almost sinister. Part of the effect was achieved by enormous antiquated cabin trunks brooding like haunted Bavarian castles in every corner. They cut down the space and increased the gloom at a stroke. They undoubtedly made the von Schreibers feel at home; their home was probably dominated by dark and hulking Biedermeyer furniture.

Joan moved uneasily through the shadows, snapping on every light. She laid out the tent that served as Frau von Schreiber's nightdress and the dark tailored pyjamas that, with minor adjustments, could serve as a uniform for Herr von Schreiber . . . Tuck the trouser legs into the tops of jackboots, add a Swastika armband over one sleeve . . . She pulled her thought away abruptly.

Still, they were an odd pair to be on the *Empress Josephine*. Apart from the food, they had not appeared to be enjoying the cruise, even before the trouble started. They paced the deck on morning constitutionals as though it were a painful duty before collapsing gratefully into deckchairs from which they stirred only to answer the ripple of chimes announcing another meal.

Herr von Schreiber had been heard to mutter at one point that this was a business trip for them and their behaviour seemed to prove it. But what kind of business? Joan remembered Jacques's theory that they were escaped Nazis reverting to type.

Certainly they both carried South American passports; she had found them when she had searched the suite. Although they did not attempt to disguise their German origin, they were to-day citizens of a country notorious for its hospitality to people who had left Germany in a hurry — and who could never go back. The Statute of Limitations on war crimes would never run out and age was no protection against the retribution that awaited.

With a shudder, Joan snapped off the overhead lights and closed the door behind her. Again she hesitated. The guard was leaning against the wall outside Mr Smithers's stateroom, it would not be strictly necessary to go in there.

However, the alternative was attending to Mrs Anson-Pryce's stateroom and she did not like the idea of going in there, even though Mrs Anson-Pryce would presumably still be at her bridge table right now.

Dave, the guard, looked up and nodded companionably. 'Everything all right?' she asked, walking towards him.

'Hope so.' He nodded towards the cabin door. 'He's gone so

quiet in there, he's either passed out or dead —' With a grimace, he acknowledged the tactlessness of the remark.

Joan sent him a token smile in response, but unease stirred within her. Smithers was, thank heaven, a happy drunk, not a nasty or quarrelsome one. He was usually singing to himself, or muttering, or trying to urge good-fellowship upon reluctant victims. It was most unlike him to settle down quietly when he had a captive audience right outside his door, someone who might be persuaded into conviviality.

'Mr Smithers?' Joan tapped on the door. 'Mr Smithers?' There was no response.

'I think I'll just check.' She turned the master key and swung open the door. The cabin was brightly lit — and empty.

'Oh my God!' Dave paled. 'He's on the loose!'

'I'm afraid so.' Joan crossed the cabin and tapped at the bathroom door before opening it. There was just a chance that he might have fallen asleep in the bath. He hadn't. 'Yes,' she confirmed. 'He's gone.'

'But how did he get out?' The guard looked wildly towards the porthole. It was closed and bolted. 'I've been outside every minute —'

'Except . . .' she said forebodingly.

'Well, I was only gone for a minute, maybe two.' He was instantly on the defensive. 'I had to take a leak. I couldn't help it. Who'd think he could get away so fast?'

'Never mind.' She picked up the telephone and dialled the Purser's Office. 'We'll catch up with him.'

Mrs Anson-Pryce surveyed the midnight buffet with approval. It had been quite a pleasant evening, after all. Not least because she, as one of the table nearest the tragedy, was known to have been an eye-witness to the whole affair. Naturally, her bridge table had wanted a full report, which she had given them, obligingly raising her voice so that the players at nearby tables had been able to listen to all the details. Some of them had joined in the questioning.

All in all, not much bridge had been played, but it had been a most satisfactory few hours. Even the odious Madge had been less irritating than usual, listening raptly to the story and gasping in all the right places.

Absently Mrs Anson-Pryce took a plate and stretched out her hand towards the small brown triangles containing smoked salmon. Two things happened at that same instant: she was rudely jostled from behind and she caught just the faintest whiff of — could it be? — bitter almonds.

Her appetite disappeared. She stepped aside and let the too-eager passenger take her place. He hadn't bothered with a plate, he grabbed a handful of triangles and crammed them into his mouth greedily.

'Disgusting!' she murmured, conscious of a slight sense of relief. It must have been the drink she had smelled. As usual, it surrounded the Smithers creature in an almost visible aura. He might even have been drinking some of that peach kernel liqueur that tasted of almonds. It was clear that he was not selective about his drink; if a liquid had any alcoholic content, he drank it. In a different social strata, he'd have been on meths.

'Hungry —' He had heard her and half-turned to apologize. 'No dinner . . . everybody left me . . . and they took the food away.' He turned back for another handful of sandwiches. 'Locked me in my cabin,' he complained bitterly.

'Yes, well . . .' Mrs Anson-Pryce edged away. The early floor show in the night club had ended and the buffet was becoming crowded. She was able to lose herself among the influx of newcomers.

Not that D. D. Smithers had any interest in retaining her company. The food was his main focus for concern. He worked his way from one end of the buffet to the other, heedless of the people jostling him as they reached around him for the delicacies on offer.

'*Isn't that* —?' His ears preternaturally attuned to the danger, he caught the *sotto voce* remark from one of the stewards bringing in a tray of fruit. They had spotted him.

Catching up a dish of chicken drumsticks, D-and-D dived through the doorway and ran down the corridor, skidding round the first turn, then the next.

When the steward reached the doorway, he was nowhere in sight.

Daniels set down the telephone and rubbed his aching head. Despite all their precautions, passenger D. D. Smithers was on the loose again and a menace to himself, if no one else. It was unlikely that D-and-D was the murderer, but it was highly probable that he was being stalked by the killer because he had not died with the rest of his table. A killer who needed to make good his boast that six would die; a killer who was no less psychotic for being mercenary with it.

Right now, one lone dipsomaniac was the least of his troubles, although Smithers would have to be found and re-incarcerated for his own safety.

More important was the destination of the *Empress Josephine*. Despite the order from the Head Office, they could not turn around and retrace their route, keeping everyone on board for another six or eight days. Permission must be sought to divert to another port. Unfortunately, Nhumbala was the nearest and going elsewhere might mean losing the time they had gained by speeding up the engines.

And then what? They were no closer to finding the maniac who had disposed of so many. Could they stand by and let all the passengers walk off the ship, knowing that one of them was a mass murderer?

Captain Falcon wouldn't like it, but they might have to admit defeat and stand-to offshore while a launch brought out police officials from shore who, knowing neither the ship nor the passengers, would most probably be as useless as any of the ship's officers at discovering the identity of the guilty party.

His headache was worsening and he could not give in to it. Daniels picked up the receiver and dialled the Doctor's Office. He needed something stronger than aspirin — and he needed something to keep him awake and alert. There was no time to waste sleeping.

No answer. He slammed down the receiver, cursing. Parker was never around when you wanted him. What did he do with himself? There was going to be an accounting demanded soon.

Never mind. On with the battle. Perhaps Sparks had been able to get back to Head Office and give them some idea of the problems on board. With luck, he might have impressed upon them the desperation of the *Empress Josephine*'s plight and the urgency of the request for all possible information on passengers and crew. Head Office might have to work through police channels to find the information, but surely they would not hesitate to do so when so much was at stake.

Had they started yet? It was time for an update on that situation.

Daniels pushed open the door of the Radio Room and stood in the doorway, stunned.

'No!' he choked. 'No!'

Sparks lay sprawled on the floor, his face cyanosed and contorted. He had been strangled. Around him lay pieces of equipment, smashed to smithereens.

The Radio Room was wrecked, the radio operator dead. There would be no more messages in or out.

The *Empress Josephine* was on her own.

CHAPTER 11

'It is positively disgraceful!' Mrs Anson-Pryce trumpeted at the breakfast table. 'When I went down to my cabin last night, the bed had not yet been turned down and the light had not been lit. The service aboard this ship is deteriorating by the moment! I shall definitely complain to the Owners of the Line!'

'Our stateroom was in perfect order,' Herr von Schreiber said coldly. 'Are you certain you are correct?'

'He is right,' Frau von Schreiber said. 'We have never found anything wrong with the service. Everyone is most friendly and efficient.'

The Ordways and the Lawtons exchanged glances. Mary hoped the morning wasn't going to start with more unpleasantness, but it was quite obvious that Hallie wouldn't mind if her table companions came to blows. She winked at Mary.

'After what happened last night,' Hallie said provocatively, 'I don't see how you can think everybody is so perfect. *I* wouldn't call it efficient to fill a water pitcher with something that made a whole table keel over —' She gave one of her inane little giggles. 'It wasn't very friendly, either.'

'Precisely!' Mrs Anson-Pryce looked rather surprised at support from such an unexpected quarter, but accepted it since it bore out her contention. 'There is something very wrong about this ship and I think it time we got to the bottom of it.'

'Wrong?' Herr von Schreiber frowned darkly. 'Last night was unfortunate, yes. But I am sure those people soon will be well again.'

'Will they?' Mrs Anson-Pryce glanced over her shoulder. The table in question had disappeared, the other tables had been rearranged to take up the space. She shivered involuntarily. It reminded her of something, something she instinctively knew she would rather not think about.

'I wouldn't like to bet we'd ever see them again,' Hallie Ordway said. 'If you ask me, they were goners.'

'You exaggerate —' Herr von Schreiber began.

'She's right!' Mrs Anson-Pryce had remembered the hasty rearrangement of the bridge tables — a 'temporary measure' until her companions of the first evening had recovered from their 'indisposition'. She had never seen them again. 'There are entirely too many people dropping out of sight aboard this vessel. I think it's high time we demanded an explanation!'

'You're right,' Hallie said. 'We should have, like, a deputation to the Captain. Either official, or when he joins the table for dinner tonight. And I think you ought to be spokesperson. You do it so well.'

'Well . . .' Mrs Anson-Pryce glanced around the table, bridling modestly. 'If everyone agrees . . .'

'Sure thing,' Mortimer Ordway said. 'Hallie's put her finger on it again. You're just the person.'

'I *have* chaired several Committees in my time . . .'

'*I* certainly wouldn't want to do it,' Mary Lawton said; she could already feel Captain Falcon's hostile eye on her. Her husband nodded agreement.

'You must do as you see fit.' Herr von Schreiber shrugged. 'I will have no part of it.'

'We should call on the Captain this morning,' Mrs Anson-Pryce said firmly. 'Later, everyone will be getting ready for the Fancy Dress Ball and we won't have his full attention.' She swept the Ordways and the Lawtons with a commanding glance. 'You'll come with me, of course.'

'Sure,' Mortie agreed. 'Anything you say. But shouldn't we collect a few other people, too? Otherwise, it will look kinda pointed, since we're all from his own table.'

'Quite right,' Mrs Anson-Pryce said. 'I'll speak to the people at my bridge table. I'm sure they'll join us.'

'And there are a couple of gals from the Keep-Fit Class who've been getting worried since someone disappeared from their table,' Hallie said. 'I'll go and find them. I know they'll want to come along.'

'Excellent,' Mrs Anson-Pryce approved. 'Then I suggest we all meet in the library at ten-thirty for a conference. I'll make an appointment to see the Captain at eleven.'

D-and-D Smithers had escaped and almost immediately afterwards, Sparks had been murdered. That proved it, didn't it?

Pesky Calhoun prowled below decks, following the cold trail. Ahead where the corridor curved, a chicken bone lay like a gypsy sign to show the fork in the road the caravan had followed.

'Come on,' Pesky said. 'He's gone that way.'

'Pesky —' Cosmo hung back. 'Are you sure this is a good idea? If he *is* the murderer, I mean? We haven't told anyone where we're going and —'

'And he's deadly and desperate,' Connie finished drily. Cosmo had tried to leave her behind when Pesky approached him about this expedition, but she had held him to their pact. They stayed together. If he was walking into danger, she was walking in with him. At the same time, she couldn't seriously view D-and-D Smithers as an insane menace, despite Pesky's insistence, so they were probably safer chasing after him than they would be up in the public lounges where the passengers — and the real killer — were milling about.

'What are you talking about?' Pesky was indignant. 'There's three of us. With weapons.'

Cosmo looked down unhappily at the object in his hand. He wouldn't call it a weapon. It was one of the special Indian clubs he and Connie had bought to practise a new juggling act — before they realised a rolling ship wasn't the best environment in which to work on something that required delicate balance. Furthermore, the clubs were of light balsa wood and, although weighted, they were not weighted heavily enough to do any harm if they accidentally struck someone — you didn't want to be knocked cold in the middle of your act if you missed a catch. The only way the Indian club could possibly be classed as a weapon would be if someone were to die laughing when threatened with it.

'What will we do with him if we find him?'

Cosmo didn't blame Connie for being sceptical, but Pesky turned and gave her a dirty look.

'We take him into custody,' Pesky said. '*Our* custody. And we march him upstairs and straight into the brig. Did you know there's a brig on this ship?'

Wordlessly, both Cosmo and Connie shook their heads.

'Well, there is. There's a brig on every ship, although they keep it quiet. They use it for any trouble with the crew and, once in a while, for a stowaway. It's up top, just before you go out to the kennels. There's a regular door on the outside, to keep it inconspicuous but, behind that, there's a real cell door — bars and all.'

'I didn't know we had a kennels abroad,' Cosmo said.

'We aren't using it this trip,' Pesky said. 'Not many cruise passengers worry about taking their pets along. It's only when they're moving from one country to another that dear little Fido or Fluffikins gets to go along.'

'I'll bet we've got a stowaway aboard this trip.' Connie went to the heart of the matter. 'Who else could be doing all this?'

'D-and-D, that's who,' Pesky said darkly. 'He's got a great cover with that drunk act, but he can't fool me. He's always around when something happens.' They had reached the end of the corridor, Pesky looked around and glimpsed another chicken bone at the curve of the stairwell. 'He's gone down here. Come on!' He plunged down the stairs.

Reluctantly, Cosmo and Connie followed. The staircase led below the passenger decks down into the bowels of the ship. The overhead lights were dimmer, the throb of the engines louder, the motion of the ship more noticeable. It was unfamiliar territory — alien and unwelcoming.

Ahead of them, Pesky moved unheedingly along the narrow companionway. They saw him halt as he came to another door and look around, then pounce on a splintered bone caught in the door frame.

'Through here —' he called, pushing open the door.

It led into a section of the cargo hold. Packing crates loomed over narrow aisles, the lights were dimmer yet. The atmosphere was dark and brooding. Anything could be waiting around any corner.

'Cosmo —' Connie caught at his sleeve as he stepped over the bulkhead; he turned back to her. 'Cosmo, I love you.'

'Me, too,' he said. 'I mean, I love you, too.' He pulled her into his arms; they clung together, kissing wildly.

'For God's sake!' Pesky said in disgust. 'This isn't the time or place for *that*. Come on, you two!'

They broke apart and followed him, still holding hands. The engines were loud enough in here to give you a headache. The ocean seemed perilously close, just beneath your feet, although Connie knew that there must still be another deck or two before the hull curved into the sharp prow that cut through the water. Momentarily she visualized it cutting through the waves ahead, the foam running back along both sides of the ship, the long broad wake behind them . . . the bodies spinning down to the ocean floor . . .

Not now. She tried to pull herself together. The latest bodies were on board because they could no longer afford to slow the ship down to the almost-halt that would allow a decent burial. The bodies were stored away somewhere on board . . .

No! They couldn't be down here. It was too hot. She shivered.

'Cold?' Cosmo asked incredulously as she shuddered. It must be ten degrees hotter down here. The smell of the oil was thick and heavy, enough to make your stomach heave. Over all, was another smell, curiously familiar and out of place here.

Pesky sniffed like a bloodhound and turned sharply at the end of the aisle. 'He's down here,' he said. 'He's somewhere close. I know it.'

Connie's hand tightened in Cosmo's clasp. They both took a firmer grip on their Indian clubs. Suddenly, they were no longer so sure that D-and-D might be innocent. Pesky's suspicion was contagious — and they had been led, slyly and secretly, away from the comparative safety of the upper decks where they had been surrounded by the ship's company and passengers, down into the depths of the hold, where there were no witnesses to what might happen to them.

'Aha —!' Ahead of them, Pesky pounced on something at the opening of another aisle. He straightened up, flourishing a greasy platter with one partially-gnawed drumstick sliding around on it. 'We've got him now! Down here!'

Instinctively they halted, meeting each other's eyes — and knew that they were not so certain they could trust Pesky. He was the one who had led them down here, insisting that no one else must know. He could have planted the greasy trail himself. This was the day on which the killer had pledged himself to account for seven more victims if his demands were not met — and he had kept his pledges so far. Were they destined to be the next victims?

'Whoever's been doing this —' Cosmo muttered uneasily — 'must be somebody with a pretty good idea of shipboard routine . . .'

'Come on!' Pesky called. The irritation in his voice sounded natural. If he were truly innocent and realized that they were suspecting him, his wrath would be monumental — and justified. He was still carrying the heavy platter which would, after all, make a better weapon than the Indian clubs.

Unless he had a still better weapon waiting down there in the corner he was leading them to. Were they walking into a trap?

'Connie —' Cosmo looked down at her, his throat aching with tenderness. 'I love you, Connie.'

'Me, too, Cosmo. I mean, I love you, too.' She squeezed his hand and, after a brief loving skirmish, was forced to allow him to precede her down the aisle since it was too narrow to walk side by side.

Connie looked up fearfully at the packing crates towering above them. Was it her imagination that they seemed to be swaying with the motion of the ship? How secure were they? Had someone — had Pesky? — loosened whatever held them in place, so that they would need only a small push to come toppling down on anyone beneath?

She saw Cosmo's head twist and turn upwards and knew that he was keeping pace with her own thoughts. How beautifully they were settling down to being an old married couple. How sad if this were to be the end of it all.

'Gotcha!' Pesky's triumphant shout rang out suddenly. It had to be genuine — he wasn't that good an actor. Not unless he had been fooling everyone all along. In which case, he outclassed Gielgud, Olivier and the top twenty greatest actors of all time rolled into one.

'Oh no — not you again!' The slurred protesting voice was unmistakable. ' 'Sno peace anywhere!'

They hurried forward to find Pesky looming menacingly over a recumbent D-and-D. As D-and-D looked up and saw Connie, he attempted to struggle to his feet. Pesky pushed him back.

'You stay just where you are. You can't try any funny business from that position. We've got you dead to rights!'

'Only havin' a l'il drink.' D-and-D was aggrieved. 'Wanna ask the l'il lady to join me. Not you — you're not friendly.'

'Damned right I'm not!' Pesky glared down at him. 'And never mind the little lady — she isn't feeling very friendly towards you, either.'

'Let'er speak for herself. She's not even *your* l'il lady. You can't tell her what to do.' He beamed an enticing smile up at Connie. 'Come'n sit down'n have a drink.' He waved a bottle at her, then another. 'Have a bourbon . . . have a brandy . . . have a scotch . . . or maybe gin . . . ?' He was surrounded by bottles.

'Where did he get all that drink?' Cosmo asked. 'He couldn't have carried all that down here by himself.'

'That's right.' Connie sank to the floor and spoke coaxingly. 'I'd love to have a drink with you, Mr Smithers, but where are the glasses? And where did you find all these lovely bottles?'

'Found the sixth bar —' D-and-D gave her a beatific smile. 'My offisher frien' showed me the way. Knew he would. 'F I followed him long enough. 'S'informal bar, though —' He patted the crate he was propped up against. 'Self-service.'

'What the hell!' Pesky squatted to take a closer look at the crate. It was stencilled 'DRIED MILK'. 'I don't believe it!' He pushed D-and-D to one side. The broken boards were now revealed. He thrust his hand inside and pulled out a bottle of twelve-year-old Kentucky bourbon.

'No need to get rough, ol' boy. Plenty there for all of us. But —' he blinked earnestly at Connie. 'No glasses, jus' bottles. Sorry. Bring your own glasses. But —' He waved his hand expansively. 'We've got thousands o' bottles.'

'Christ Almighty!' Pesky straightened up with a haunted look. He darted to a packing crate stencilled 'FAMINE RELIEF'. 'Give me a hand, Cosmo,' he ordered; he was tearing at the packing crate with his bare hands.

'Wait a minute —' Cosmo dug in his pocket for the Swiss Army knife he'd bought before leaving New York. Connie had teased him about it, but if the ship had sunk and they had wound up on a desert island, they'd be very glad to have it. It was useful now. Cosmo found a gadget that could be used for prying up nails and set to work.

'Gin!' Pesky clawed out a bottle and looked at it in despair. 'It's a crateful of gin!'

'Coulda told you that, ol' boy,' D-and-D said. 'FAMINE's gin an' scotch. DRIED MILK's bourbon an' brandy. Simple!'

'Simple!' Pesky looked around wildly. 'What about the big crates? The ones marked "MEDICAL SUPPLIES"?'

'Very boring, ol' boy,' D-and-D assured him. 'Nothing interesting in *them*.'

Cosmo was already working on a MEDICAL SUPPLIES crate; it was bigger than the other crates. He and Pesky exchanged worried looks, firmly on the same side now. What D-and-D considered uninteresting was not necessarily so.

As soon as the first slat was prised up far enough, Pesky reached in and fumbled around in the crate. His face changed as his hand encountered something. He grasped and pulled; he had gone pale.

'Jesus!' The long thin barrel of a rifle slid into view.

'Tol' you so, ol' boy. Nothing we care about in *those* crates.' With a final beatific smile, D-and-D leaned back and passed out of the picture.

'This one —' Pesky pointed to another large crate of "MEDICAL SUPPLIES". 'Check this one! They can't *all* hold rifles.'

'You're right.' Cosmo checked. 'This one's got machine-guns.'

'Holy hell!' Pesky wiped his perspiring forehead with a shaking hand. 'When we get to Nhumbala, we could all be jailed for about a hundred years apiece. This ship is loaded to the gunwales with contraband cargo!'

CHAPTER 12

Captain Falcon ground his teeth and tried to look as though he cared what the passengers were talking about. Blithering land-lubbers, to the last man — and woman. None of them knew what they were talking about. Of course, if they did know, they might be leaping overboard.

The happy picture curved his mouth and gave his visage the most pleasant expression it had shown since the delegation was ushered into his office.

'Furthermore —' Mrs Anson-Pryce was emboldened by this suggestion of sympathy. 'I really must point out that my stewardess is neglecting her duty shockingly. Not only that, I have reason to believe that she drinks like a fish. I've seen her first thing in the morning and she *reeks* of it!'

If you knew what she knows, madam, you might take to drink, too. He could not say it, of course. His jaw twitched with the effort of holding back the words — and all the other words he'd like to blast these pettifogging nincompoops with.

'You must remember —' Carl Daniels cut in hastily — 'the staff hours are quite different from yours. She'll have been on duty most of the night. The first thing in the morning to you is the end of a long day to her. Any drink she takes is the equivalent of a nightcap before she goes off duty and gets some sleep.'

Captain Falcon shot Daniels a moderately grateful look. It would do these passengers good to be told a few home truths, but he was reluctantly aware that discretion forbade such a course.

'We don't mean to be difficult,' Mortimer Ordway said apologetically. 'But we're not dumb. We can see there's something awfully wrong around here. We think we have a right to be told.'

'If you don't tell us,' Hallie put in, 'people are only going to start guessing — and that might be even worse.'

'Precisely!' Mrs Anson-Pryce regained her position as spokesperson and shot the Ordways a quelling glance. 'Just what I was about to point out. Rumours are already circulating — quite shocking rumours.'

Oh, for the good old days when no one questioned the Captain's authority; when passengers knew their place — and what that place would be if they upset the Master of the Ship. Oh, for the cat-o'-nine-tails, the keelhauling, the marooning on a desert island!

'We *are* in a rather tenuous position at the moment —' Seeing danger flash in the Captain's eyes, Daniels stepped in smoothly to try to defuse the situation. 'The fact is, there's been a revolution in Nhumbala. We don't know how serious it is yet, but it may be necessary for us to divert to another port.'

'Another port!' There were gasps of consternation. As he had hoped, the prospect of changing destinations sidetracked them from the original issue.

'A revolution?' Mrs Anson-Pryce glared at the Captain as though he had been personally responsible. 'Have the rebels captured the entire country or just the port?'

'We don't know yet,' Daniels answered. 'We're trying to get more information now, but the situation's pretty confused. As soon as we know something definite, there'll be an official announcement.'

'And when will that be?'

When — and if — the Chief Electrician and the mechanic managed to repair the smashed radio equipment and put the ship back into contact with the world again.

'As soon as possible, but we can't be definite. You know how it is with revolutions — the situation changes minute to minute. We'll let you know when we can make a decision.'

'My ticket is to Nhumbala,' Mrs Anson-Pryce said coldly,

'and that is where I must go. If the country is in the throes of a revolution, then it is even more imperative that I should be there to look after my business interests.'

'I quite understand that,' Daniels said. 'I promise, we'll do our best to get you there. However, if the safety of the ship and passengers —'

'Yeah, what about us?' Hallie was indignant. 'This isn't the kind of prize the quiz show meant to give us. The Cruise of a Lifetime, they called it — and people are dying all around us! How about that?'

'Quite so,' Mrs Anson-Pryce cut in quickly, trying to cover her lapse. In the light of the information about the revolution, she had forgotten the original purpose of the delegation.

'That's an exaggeration, Mrs Ordway.' Daniels wondered how much they knew and how much they had guessed. The deaths in the dining salon were the only ones they had witnessed; he had to assume that they didn't know about the other deaths. 'We had a great tragedy last night, but —'

'But was that the only one? We need to know. Why, I'm half way afraid to eat or drink anything any more. It wouldn't surprise me,' Hallie added darkly, 'if the TV company didn't ask for their money back after we tell them about this trip!'

There were murmurs of agreement from everyone except Mrs Anson-Pryce, who was beginning to wonder just which one was spokesperson around here.

'A great tragedy —' Daniels took a deep breath and began lying. 'However, we have investigated and I'm glad to say that we have now sorted out the problem. Nothing like that will ever occur again. The situation is under control —'

The door burst open. Kicked open.

Captain Falcon rose to his feet in a fury and found himself looking into the blazing eyes of that damned disruptive dining-room steward.

'How dare you burst in here like that? You knock before you enter the Captain's quarters —'

'You are no longer the Captain.' Edgar swaggered into the

office, trailed by two of the Nhumbalan girl croupiers. All three carried machine-guns with varying degrees of ease.

'I am hereby taking command of this ship in the name of the people of Nhumbala. I am Captain now!'

Dr Parker stepped back from the bedside and met Joan's eyes. He shook his head and gently lifted the sheet, pulling it up to cover the quiet face. *You can't win them all.* But that was not a remark he could make with a widow still at the bedside.

'I'm sorry,' he said instead. 'Very sorry, Mrs Baldwin.'

'You did all you could.' She raised her head, eyes glittering with the tears about to fall. 'We knew this might be our last trip together. It was going to happen, sooner or later, and we decided we wanted to be out doing things and having fun rather than sitting around counting his heartbeats and waiting . . .'

The tears came and Joan moved forward to comfort her. Parker found a sedative and retreated to the bathroom to get a glass of water.

The woman took the capsule absently, no longer with them except in body; her work of mourning had begun. There was little they could do for her.

'Another cabin?' Parker suggested to Joan. 'You could move her now so that —' *So that she wouldn't be here when the crew came to remove the body.*

'No!' The thought, as much as the words, had penetrated the woman's daze. She raised her head defiantly. 'I want to stay here with him. I don't want another cabin.'

'All right, just as you like.' Parker nodded soothingly and fell back a few steps.

She bowed her head and reverted to immobility, staring unseeingly at the figure beneath the sheet.

'Stay with her,' he said to Joan quietly. 'Keep an eye on her until the sedative starts working. We don't want to lose another one.'

'Jack —' Joan had followed him to the door, she caught his arm. 'Jack, I suppose it really was a heart attack? It wasn't —?'

'It was a genuine heart attack,' he said wearily. 'You heard Mrs Baldwin — there was a long case history. They were expecting it.' From the depths of his exhaustion, he dredged up a weak smile.

'People *do* die naturally,' he assured her. 'Even on board *this* ship.'

'Throw that man in irons!' Captain Falcon bellowed. 'The women, too!' If they wanted equality, they could have it.

For a frozen moment, no one moved. Edgar still dominated the room — or tried to — but this wasn't the reception he had expected. Behind him, the girls flustered visibly, their guns swaying and dipping; they were not committed revolutionaries.

'I give the orders!' Edgar said, not quite convincingly. He flourished his machine-gun and seemed nonplussed when it did not inspire the terror he had calculated upon.

'This is *too* much!' Mrs Anson-Pryce said in exasperation. 'Captain Falcon, *do* something!'

As though her words had released them from a spell, several people started forward. In the face of such concerted threat, the intruders moved together, back to back, and brought up their guns, ready to begin the circling-and-shooting manœuvre so familiar to terrorists.

Without moving from her spot, Hallie Ordway kicked out in the same high-kick she had used to kick the top hat off the compère's head in the quiz show. Her foot connected with the machine-gun so nervously held by the nearest girl and sent it spinning to the far corner of the room.

As Edgar turned his head to see what had happened, Mortimer Ordway dived at his knees and brought him down in a flying tackle. Reflex action sent a burst of bullets into the ceiling before the gun dropped.

Simultaneously, Daniels stepped forward and removed the machine-gun from the unresisting hands of the stupefied girl who was staring at her companions in bewilderment. How had it all gone so wrong, so quickly? People were supposed to be at the mercy of those who held guns, quaking and terrified, not fighting back; not winning.

The machine-gun fire had brought every crew member within earshot running to help. They crowded into the office surrounding the sullen and defeated rebels, taking them captive.

'Mrs Ordway, Mr Ordway —' Captain Falcon shook their hands. 'We owe you a debt of gratitude. Your prompt action —'

'Well, hell!' Mortimer Ordway cut him off. 'It was the least we could do. We don't want those characters taking over the ship. I figure we've got problems enough.'

Chimes rippled out from the loudspeaker system, announcing lunch. Instinctively the heads of the delegation turned towards the sound.

'There you are,' Captain Falcon said thankfully. 'Time for lunch. Our troubles are now over, I'm happy to say. Some of you may recognize Edgar — he was a dining-room steward. We've got him in custody — and we'll keep him there. You can eat and drink safely from now on. As our friend, Jacques, would say; "*Bon appétit.*" '

The two parties nearly collided outside the brig. Pesky, Cosmo and Connie, reinforced by First Officer Hanson and the Chief Engineer had just slammed the door of one of the two small cells on D-and-D when Edgar's captors, led by Captain Falcon and Carl Daniels, reached the brig and stopped outside, staring blankly at the captive already incarcerated therein.

'*Hail, hail, th' gang's all here* . . .' D-and-D greeted them blithely. 'More th'merrier, an'all that . . .' He looked at Edgar curiously. 'What've *you* been up to, ol' boy?'

'Don't trust him!' Pesky said. 'Don't take your eyes off him! Don't let him take you in — he's trouble all the way! Every time anybody dies, he's near by. You can't tell *me* he's just an innocent bystander!'

'Thass not a frien'ly thing to say, ol' boy.' D-and-D stared at him reproachfully.

'Never mind that,' Pesky snarled. 'We've got you locked up now — and we're going to throw away the key!'

'Take it easy, fella.' Mortimer Ordway, obviously reluctant to relinquish his moment of glory, could not be shaken off and had accompanied them to the brig to lock up Edgar, while his wife went with the other half of the party to see the female rebels locked into their cabin. 'It's over now, fella. *We've* got the guilty party right here.'

'The hell you have! *I've* caught the guilty one!'

'I'm innocent,' D-and-D pleaded through the bars. 'Thought it was a self-service cocktail lounge, thass all. Bit rough'n ready, but thought it was for th'crew. Didn't mean to steal the liquor. Look —' he pulled a handful of cash from his pocket — 'Perfec-'ly willin' to pay for everything.'

'I am not guilty of anything!' Edgar declared. 'My position is plain. I am the rightful Captain of this ship in the name of the people of Nhumbala!'

'Throw him inside!' Captain Falcon snarled. 'Keep them both locked up while we sort this out. For all we know, they're both in it together. I'll question them later.' He'd give them a good long time to cool their heels and get worried. Tomorrow was time enough, then he'd start with the women.

'Captain —' Pesky was suddenly reminded. 'I've got to talk to you in private.' He glanced at Edgar, at the captured machine-guns some of the crew were still holding. 'About the cargo.'

'Cargo?' The note in Pesky's voice alerted Captain Falcon. There was more unpleasantness on the way.

The other cell door clanged, the key turned.

'Cellmate! Or almos' . . .' D-and-D greeted the new arrival. 'Won't be lonely any more. If you've got a pack of cards, we can —'

Edgar gave him a black look, retreated to the farthest corner of his own cell and stood with his face to the wall.

'Oh, no! He's not fren'ly, either,' D-and-D mourned. 'Never gonna travel on this ship again —'

The outside wooden door slammed shut, cutting off his plaint.

By the time lunch was over, everyone was aware that the madman responsible for the outrage in the dining salon had been caught and locked up. It was terrible, it was tragic, but it was over.

A new spirit of festivity pervaded the ship. Buoyant with relief, the passengers prepared to excel each other at the Fancy Dress Ball. Stewards and stewardesses were called into consultation; unlikely conspiracies flourished; passengers fluttered about like magpies, collecting strange items of equipment and bits of anything that glittered. They passed each other giggling in the corridors, trying to conceal oddly shaped parcels and pieces of brightly coloured materials. Laughter bubbled amid excited whispers. Suddenly the *Empress Josephine* was *en fête* — as she should have been all through the voyage.

Joan quickened her steps as she saw the red bulb alight over the von Schreibers' door. She had not heard their buzzer, but she had not been at her post for quite a while. There was too much to do with so many passengers entering into the spirit of the impending occasion and all determined to compete for the prizes.

It would be nice if she could summon up any festive spirit herself, but she had sat with Mrs Baldwin until the new widow had fallen asleep. It had taken a long while and she had had to listen to reminiscences of the happy marriage so abruptly ended. She felt dull and heavy with the weight of someone else's memories — and pain.

It was great relief that the killer had been caught. Strange that it had been Edgar . . . somehow, she wouldn't have thought him capable . . . but death still brooded over this voyage. Natural death was no less final and fearsome than the unnatural deaths — the murders. People could still die of natural causes before the ship docked. And the von Schreibers were elderly and very overweight, ripe for trouble.

She tapped nervously on the door and was relieved to hear Frau von Schreiber's placid tone bidding her to enter.

'You rang?' Joan reached up automatically and switched off the red signal light as she stepped into the stateroom.

'*Ja.*' Frau von Schreiber was unfolding a voluminous white garment. 'I require three bunches of grapes. Purple grapes. Large bunches.'

'Purple grapes?' Joan looked at her blankly.

'Green will have to do if the purple are not available. But the purple are better.' Frau von Schreiber shook out the garment and regarded it with approval. It was now revealed as a vaguely Grecian costume.

'Oh, I see,' Joan said. 'It's for the Fancy Dress Ball.'

'*Ja!*' Frau von Schreiber looked at her with unexpectedly twinkling eyes. 'I go as a Bacchante. I always go as a Bacchante. I have the costume made a long time ago und I always pack it.' She dived into one of the trunks again and surfaced clutching some dark green shapes and streamers.

'The vine leaves also I pack,' she confided. 'Vun cannot be certain of finding vine leaves on any but Greek ships, so I bring mine own. But the purple grapes I need.'

'Of course.' Joan felt a genuine smile begin to curve her lips. It was possible that the world might become an amusing place again some day. 'I'll get you some purple grapes right away.'

'Three bunches, mind you. I vear them *here, here* und *here.*' She wriggled skittishly. 'Und mein Otto eats them after der Ball for a bedtime snack!'

At least they were going to feed him this time. If you could call it food. He gazed at the tray without enthusiasm. It was a large bowl of some sort of goulash, accompanied only by a spoon. The rolls were already buttered. There was no drink — not even wine.

D-and-D slewed his gaze sideways to inspect the tray that had been slid into the adjoining cell. Same menu — or lack of it. Prisoners can't be choosers. Silly not to let them have butter knives — what did they think anyone could do with them?

Wonder they hadn't taken away their shoe-laces and belts. Absently, he checked himself. No, he was still wearing those items.

His head was aching. He needed another drink. Gotta keep topped up. Hair of the dog that bit him an' all that. Don' feel right, otherwise. Alcohol level goes down an' a man starts feeling all sorts of aches and pains he didn't notice before. Physical and mental.

Ol' joke, wasn't there? 'I drink to forget.' 'What do you want to forget?' 'I can't remember.'

Only he remembered, every now and again. Now especially. It was today, wasn't it? Today or tomorrow. His only daughter would be walking down the aisle — on the arm of her uncle. Given away by her uncle, his wife's brother.

Marsha had packed him off on this trip so that he wouldn't be there to embarrass her. Embarrass them all.

Didn't want to divorce him. She knew the statistical tables. Why settle for a piddling alimony when, with a few more years and a bit of luck, he'd drink himself into the grave and she'd have it all. Long as she hung on. But she didn't want to put up with him any more than she had to. Not on important occasions, when the cream of society — slightly curdled, what passed for it in their town — was going to be present. Not wanted at the wedding.

Not wanted on the voyage, either.

The outer door opened. A hand slid through the gap. The hand held out a flask of brandy. There was crisp gold braid on a uniformed sleeve showing at the wrist. That was more like it. He had friends, after all.

D-and-D snatched the flask and looked guiltily at Edgar, who was still sunk in a deep and brooding silence, ignoring his meal, looking inward, seeing nothing but his own problem. D-and-D raised the flask to his lips and gulped greedily.

Aaah, that was more like it! The aches, the pains, the mental anguish receded. He gulped again. The peaceful familiar blur spread over his surroundings, making them more bearable.

The door opened wider, the hand appeared again. This time it held a key. That was more like it. Oh, much more like it. That was really friendly.

The outer door swung back all the way. The tall figure in tropical white uniform moved forward to insert the key into the lock of the barred door.

'Glad to see you. Thought you were never comin', ol' boy.' D-and-D blinked owlishly at the face he could not quite discern. The uniform cap was pulled low over the eyes, the other hand held a handkerchief to the face, as though about to sneeze.

Never mind. It was what was happening that was important. The cell door swung open.

Now Edgar came to life, stood up and moved forward, awaiting his turn to be released. He peered intently at the officer, frowning in puzzlement.

'You comin', ol' boy?' D-and-D paused outside his cell and waited. He was never one to discourage anyone who might be disposed to be friendly.

'You go and have a drink,' the officer said gruffly. 'He'll be along in a few minutes.'

D-and-D raised his hand in friendly salute and started off down the corridor. Another drink was a good idea, just what he needed right now. Behind him, he was only vaguely aware of the voices continuing.

'You!' Edgar choked. 'No! Keep away from me, man! . . . It can't be! You're . . .'

D-and-D had reached the stairs. He turned and descended them. He heard no more.

CHAPTER 13

It was silent and deserted in the upper gallery. The first sitting passengers had eaten and gone back to their cabins to prepare for the evening's festivities. The second sitting passengers were in the dining salon at their meal right now, after which they too would hurry to their cabins to get into their costumes, or to the Main Lounge to bag ringside seats for the Fancy Dress Ball.

Time to shut the shop. There would be no more customers tonight.

She snapped out the lights in the showcases; the sparkle of gems died to the glow of a banked fire in the dim light remaining. She turned out the window lights except for the strategically placed spotlights which would illumine the expensive centrepieces all through the night.

The overhead lights inside the shop were the last to go out. Automatically she turned to set the alarm, then was halted by a sudden tap at the door.

Not a customer. It was one of the ship's officers. He might have a message. On the other hand, he might have been sent as an errand boy (passengers recognized no hierarchy but their own) by some dowager who had decided suddenly that she must have one of the jewelled pieces on display to complete her costume for the evening.

'Yes?' She opened the door. 'What is —?'

He moved forward swiftly, hands closing around her throat, propelling her backwards into the dark shadows. Taken by surprise, overpowered, her struggles were brief.

If anyone had been watching, they might have seen the last light go out.

Then, after a long silent waiting period, a hand reached into the show window and began stripping the gems from the moulded black velvet display forms.

Daniels checked his watch, then pulled down the latticework grille closing off the Purser's Office. After a moment's reflection, he also closed the wooden shutters behind it. So long as the passengers could see through to the bank of safe-deposit boxes in which they stored their valuables, some of them would be sure that they could still gain access. It was better to be seen to be uncompromisingly closed for the night.

Or, at least, until after the Fancy Dress Ball when so many would wish to replace their jewels in the safes. The office would have to open up again for that.

It was going to be a long night.

He also had to see the Baggagemaster, who had his men checking the crates in the hold to find out just how much contraband they were carrying. Rather, to discern whether any of the cargo was legitimate at all. Then he had to question the girl croupiers and find out as much as possible before he tackled Edgar. The fact that they had all been armed with machine-guns meant that Edgar must have been responsible for the shipment. Presumably he was working for his cousin, the Dictator, in which case, there would be no problem unloading the cargo when the ship docked — if the country was still in the same hands. The *Empress Josephine* would not be the first ship to carry dubious cargo to ports such as Nhumbala. Daniels remembered the story of the Customs Official who had telephoned his own Dictator to report solemnly, 'Sir, your furniture is leaking.'

Before he faced any of those problems, however, he had to put in an appearance at the Fancy Dress Ball where he was supposed to be one of the judges.

A very long night.

'Testing . . . one . . . two . . . three . . .' Pesky adjusted the microphone fractionally and tried again. 'Testing . . . one . . . two . . . three . . . Am I coming through okay?'

'Loud and clear.' From the back of the Main Lounge, Cosmo waved an acknowledging hand.

'Just fine from where I stand.' Connie was almost out of sight behind one of the great pillars. The people who stood there wouldn't be able to see much, but they'd be able to hear all right.

'That's great.' Pesky turned to the pianist. 'You've got all the music?'

'I could do this in my sleep,' was the bored reply. After five years aboard this ship, it wouldn't be surprising if he did sleep-walk through it. It was only new and exciting for the passengers.

'Well, keep one eye open enough to match the signature tune to the costume, huh?' Pesky was irritable and nervous, the more so because he didn't know why. He'd captured D-and-D, hadn't he? And the others had captured Edgar. No matter which of them had been doing the killings, the danger was over. So why wasn't he more relaxed? Everyone else was.

Why were the hairs still prickling on the back of his neck? Why was he jumping at any sudden movement? What was he so upset about? It was all clear sailing from here on in. There was only the Fancy Dress Ball to get through and that was no big deal. Like the pianist, he could walk through it in his sleep.

The Fancy Dress — that was it. Pesky realized that, danger over or not, he did not like the idea of people roaming all over the ship in costumes. Possibly masked. Nobody able to tell who was who.

Connie stumbled as she mounted the dais, dropping the clipboard she had been carrying. It hit the dance floor with a clatter. Pesky jumped a mile.

'God damn it!' he snarled. 'Watch what you're doing!'

Joan hurried down the corridor towards the small red bulb glowing over the von Schreibers' door. She wished the Ball would start; she was run off her feet with the last-minute demands.

'Mortie — hold still!' Squeals and laughter were coming from the Ordways' suite as she passed. 'I can't help it — it tickles! I don't know how you women can . . .' There was another yelp and more laughter.

Joan was smiling as she tapped at the von Schreibers' door and swung it open.

'More grapes!' Frau von Schreiber demanded. 'I must have more grapes! Otto has been eating already, and to the Ball covered in twigs I cannot go!'

'Right away,' Joan assured her.

'He vill have stomach-ache tonight — and be served rightly!' Frau von Schreiber predicted direly to the closing door.

Mrs Anson-Pryce emerged from her stateroom as Joan hurried past. She was wearing a black velvet gown and was liberally sprinkled with diamonds; it was obvious that she was going to be one of the spectators and not one of the participants.

'Good evening.' Joan smiled automatically.

'I sincerely trust that it will be.' Mrs Anson-Pryce shot a meaningful look in the direction of Mr Smithers's empty cabin. '*Now.*'

Joan was not going to be drawn into that sort of conversation — even if she had the time. She glanced pointedly at her watch. 'You ought to be able to get a good seat, if you go up now.'

'There's no hurry.' Mrs Anson-Pryce swept past her majestically. 'The Lawtons have reserved a table and I'm joining them. We'll have a ringside seat.'

Captain Falcon received a round of applause as he led his Officers into the Main Lounge and up on to the dais where they seated themselves at the Judges' Table.

In the interests of democracy, each table on the floor also had voting forms and scribble pads. Extra tables had been brought in and were pushed together leaving a clear circle in the middle of the dance floor where the contestants could perform before the judges. After the Grand Parade at the end, the ballots would be collected, the officers would count the votes and Captain Falcon would announce the winners and present the prizes: bottles of champagne.

Waiters scurried around taking orders for drinks and returning with them at record pace. It was one of the biggest nights for the bar. It had better be. The gambling casino was 'Closed for the Evening' on the pretext that everyone would be attending the Fancy Dress Ball. There was no point in underlining the fact, to those who didn't know, that two of the three girl croupiers were under detention in a cabin below.

Outside the main entrance the extrovert gaggle in costume

giggled and pushed amiably, collecting their identifying number cards from Cosmo and Connie, who were trying to sort them into some sort of order.

Joan lingered by the entrance, enjoying the sight of someone else deep in chaos. Jacques stood just behind her and gave a silent signal to the waiters. They were to keep out of the way for the next few minutes while the revellers paraded once around the Main Lounge so that everyone could see their costumes and numbers.

'Here —' Joan had laughed too quickly. Connie thrust a packet of safety-pins at her. 'Help me pin on some numbers —'

'Okay, take it easy —' Pesky now had custody of the clipboard and was jotting down numbers and assumed identities so that he could announce them for their solo turns. 'Plenty of time. Don't worry, I'll get you all down. No. 33 — Harem Girl — great, great . . . No. 44 — no, wait a minute. You get back there, honey. I want No. 34 now. Numerical order, ladies and gentlemen, *please* . . .'

Eventually a long straggling line snaked back along the hall, through the library, with a few on the end spilling over into the cocktail bar. All were numbered and noted down, praised, and wished good luck, then Pesky went back to the microphone and the others awaited the signal to start the opening procession.

Once around the Main Lounge, out the opposite door, and then the long tedious wait while the contestants were called forward, one at a time, to cross that endless expanse of floor space 'in character' and twirl before the judges' platform. Some bolstered themselves with more drinks while they waited; inhibitions slipped away; winning was the only important thing.

Joan was always amazed at the way some of them let themselves go. Others didn't surprise her at all.

Hallie Ordway, in a very abbreviated acrobat's costume, bounced up and down excitedly, raring to go. Beside her, Mortie was wrapped in windings of toilet paper and invisible tape to become an Ancient Egyptian mummy. He wore a carefully painted mummy's mask. When he pushed the mask aside for a breath of air, Joan saw that his face had been made up with eyebrow pencil and eyeliner to duplicate the mask. Even the formal Pharaoh's beard had been affixed to his chin.

Frau von Schreiber was a not-unattractive Bacchante, but her husband was a surprise as a circus Ringmaster, complete with boots, riding whip and top hat.

'Probably the remains of his SS uniform,' Jacques growled.

'Not the top hat,' Joan protested.

'Only because he dare not wear his cap. He would be more at home in it. See, his hand keeps straying to his side in search of the holster and gun.'

Herr von Schreiber pulled a handkerchief out of his side pocket and sneezed loudly.

'You shouldn't think the worst of people, Jacques,' Joan reprimanded.

'I do not. Only of Germans. Does the leopard change its spots?'

Fanfare music sounded from the Main Lounge and the line began to shuffle forward slowly.

Captain Falcon watched with interest as the third Harem Girl in a row writhed around the dance floor, desperately trying to outdo the others. If she did that shoulder wriggle once more, she was in danger of being a topless harem dancer.

The rest of the audience wasn't quite so interested; they had seen it all before — twice. Half way across, the Harem Girl seemed to realize this and switched to an inexpert but enthusiastic version of a bellydance. Now the lower half of her costume was in danger.

Someone threw a grape. Herr von Schreiber obviously had hidden depths. Or was it his wife? Her giggle rose above the scattered applause.

Then it was Hallie's turn. She threw up her arms and posed in the doorway until every eye was on her. Then she gave a yelp of triumph and cartwheeled across the floor.

Impressive. They'd seen it before, but they loved it. They'd be able to tell all their friends that they'd seen the famous television contestant doing her famous act in person.

Hallie landed upright in front of Captain Falcon, bowed left and right, then started to circle the floor. This time she did forward somersaults to the half-way mark, then completed the round with back somersaults.

Again she stood before Captain Falcon and he joined in the applause. More bows, a few kisses thrown, then Hallie tilted forward into a handstand and slowly, carefully — her balance did not seem so assured as when she was doing the fast flips that took on their own momentum — she began to walk towards the exit on her hands.

The applause mounted, then a great roar cut across all other sounds. Heads turned to seek the source. Hallie, unconcerned, continued her slow progress across the floor.

The Mummy, stiff-legged and menacing, stalked through the doorway and advanced upon the unaware Hallie.

'Look out!' someone screamed, getting into the spirit of the act.

'Watch it!' another voice called.

'Look behind you!' They were all joining in now.

The pianist switched to 'haunted house' music. Nervous laughter mounted. Someone squealed with excitement and the Mummy paused, swung towards the noisy table, and raised his arms threateningly. They shrank back as he took a couple of steps towards them. Then he veered off and went back to his pursuit of the unsuspecting Hallie. This time no one shrieked to warn her, it had suddenly become almost real. To make a sound was to attract the Mummy's unwelcome attention to oneself.

The Mummy moved slowly but Hallie, balanced uneasily on her hands, was even slower. Pace by pace, he gained on her, loomed over her, then bent and swept her up into his arms, bearing her off in triumph while her screams rang out with all-too-lifelike horror.

The Mummy made a triumphal circuit of the dance floor, Hallie still shrieking with terror in his arms. The applause began, sporadically at first, then grew as all the tables joined in.

Captain Falcon marked his voting card judiciously. Whatever he thought of them personally, he had to admit that the Ordways had added a new dimension to the Fancy Dress Ball. They deserved some sort of prize — perhaps even First.

'Encore!' someone shouted and others took up the cry. The Mummy hesitated and turned his head from side to side in bewilderment, the light glinting off the rigid mask covering his face.

'Encore!' They were all shouting now.

Hallie obligingly tumbled out of the Mummy's arms and began backing away from him in a cowering retreat. The Mummy stumbled after her. Someone outside had the wit to dim the lights and the macabre charade took on a new dimension: it might have been happening in some newly-opened Egyptian tomb. The piano accompaniment was suitably hushed and sinister.

Predator and victim, they circled the perimeter of the dance floor one final time. Then the Mummy swooped again. Hallie's screams resounded through the lounge until, on a dying fall, she went limp and swooned in the monster's arms.

The uncertain applause began as the Mummy bore her off, moving unseeingly, but unerringly, towards the proper exit. The lights flickered and came on full again. The applause mounted.

Another scream cut through the room from the entrance. A wild-eyed woman in flowing nightdress stood in the entrance.

Why couldn't they stop copying one another? One Harem Girl was enough; one screamer was more than enough. Captain Falcon looked irritably at Pesky Calhoun, waiting for the announcement to learn whether this was supposed to be Lady Macbeth or Lucia di Lammermoor. Pesky was riffling through the pages of his scribbled programme with a frantic air, trying to find her entry.

She was crossing the floor now, sobbing. She looked as though she might want to wring her hands, but the sheet of paper she was carrying prevented this.

Music, Captain Falcon decided gloomily. She was going to give the music to the pianist and render a goddamned aria. It must be Lucia di —

'Explain that!' She hurled the piece of paper into Captain Falcon's face.

Captain Falcon caught the paper and glared at Pesky. Who was this woman? She wore no contestant's number either fore or aft. What was she doing here?

Pesky shook his head, pantomiming innocence and bewilderment. She wasn't down on the list.

'Read it! Explain it! Where's Maureen? Tell me the truth! Where are all the others?' Her voice rose hysterically.

The pianist had stopped playing. The Ordways had halted just short of the exit. Hallie slipped to the ground quietly, Mortie pushed back the Pharaoh's mask, his face underneath so blank and impassive with shock as to make no difference.

'She's dead, isn't she?' Miss O'Fallon hurled the accusation into the silence. 'You've been lying to me, keeping it from me. They're all dead! You've been deceiving everyone on board!'

CHAPTER 14

'May I see that, please, Captain?' Daniels detached the sheet of paper from Captain Falcon's nerveless grasp. Dr Parker left the dais and moved towards the hysterical woman on the floor.

'WHERE ARE THE OTHERS? DEMAND THE TRUTH! YOU HAVE A RIGHT TO KNOW. THEY ARE KILLING YOU WITH THEIR SILENCE. ARE YOUR JEWELS WORTH MORE THAN YOUR LIFE? . . .'

'Where did you get this?' Daniels demanded of Miss O'Fallon. His eye skimmed rapidly over the rest of the message. The style was familiar, but this seemed to be addressed to the passengers rather than to the Captain and Officers.

'WHERE ARE YOUR FRIENDS? LOOK AROUND YOU. WHERE ARE
THE PEOPLE YOU MET AT THE BEGINNING OF THE VOYAGE? . . .
THEY ARE DEAD. BURIED AT SEA. IN SECRET . . .'

'Where did you get this?' he shouted.

'It was pushed under my cabin door,' she quavered. 'With
the programme of tomorrow's events. Instead of the ship's
newspaper. Is it true? Is it some awful joke? What's going on?
Where's Maureen? I want to see her — I don't care if she's got
the Black Plague! I want to see her!'

'What *is* this? What's the matter?' The Ordways had come
forward and Hallie made an abortive snatch at the paper in the
Purser's hands. He pulled back just in time.

'Jack, take Miss O'Fallon to the hospital.' Their eyes met
over her head. 'Let her see her friend.'

'Just come this way —' The doctor took her arm and tried to
lead her away.

'I want to know what's going on here.' Mortimer Ordway
moved forward to block their path. He looked both incongruous
and menacing in the Mummy's wrappings. 'I think we have a
right to know.'

'That's right, you do —' Miss O'Fallon turned to him. 'It
says so right there in that paper. We all do!'

The people had risen from the tables surrounding the dance
floor and were crowding forward. The contestants were hovering uncertainly by the entrance. Outside there seemed to be a
growing commotion.

'Let's see that paper —' Mortimer Ordway tried to take it.

'All in good time.' Daniels stepped back, folding the paper
and putting it in his pocket. He sent Pesky a look of sharp
command.

'Play something!' Pesky snapped at the pianist. 'Get them
dancing. We don't want the balloon going up now.'

The pianist began playing, but was drowned out by a disturbance spreading in from the doorway.

'Come on, folks,' Pesky pleaded desperately. 'Let's have a

little dancing. And then we'll get back to the competition and see a few more contestants —'

Several people not in party dress surged across the dance floor; they seemed to be in various stages of sleeping attire. They were waving pieces of paper similar to Miss O'Fallon's. They advanced upon Captain Falcon and the officers.

It was too late for dancing; the balloon had gone up.

'I don't believe it,' Pesky said. 'There can't be any more trouble. We've got him safely locked away.' He stared down incredulously at the piece of paper someone had thrust into his hand.

The message had been pushed under every cabin door while the occupants were at, or supposedly at, the Fancy Dress Ball. To add insult to injury, it had been printed on the ship's own duplicating equipment.

In the centre of the floor the Purser was still trying to quell the uproar. Captain Falcon stepped down from the dais and shouldered his way through the crowd to stand by the Purser.

'It can't be true!' Pesky denied the evidence before his eyes. Cosmo and Connie had joined him beside the pianist, instinctively feeling safer near a spotlight and microphone. 'You saw it —' he looked at them accusingly. 'We locked him up — but they muffed it! Somehow they muffed it!'

'I opened my door right away to see where it had come from —' one of the men was saying. 'And I saw him just turning the corner. He was in uniform. One of the ship's officers. So it must be official.'

'A night like this,' someone else said, 'how can you tell? All these costumes everywhere. It coulda been anyone . . .'

'Come on!' Pesky jerked his head at Connie and Cosmo. 'Let's go and check the brig!'

'Right now?' Connie shrank back. 'Why don't we wait a while? Maybe round up some of the crew to come with us?'

'Come on!' Pesky led the way and, after an exchange of hopeless glances, Connie and Cosmo followed him.

Pesky was walking so fast they could barely keep up with him, not that they were all that anxious to. He didn't bother waiting for the lift, but charged up the stairs, only looking back when he reached the top.

'Come on . . .' But there was less irritation now and more uncertainty. Whatever was waiting behind the cell door, he did not wish to discover it by himself.

They followed. What else could they do? They couldn't desert Pesky at this point, nor were they keen on the idea of retracing their steps by themselves. Such safety as there was lay in numbers.

'Hey!' Pesky halted before the outer door and looked back at them uneasily. 'Hey, this door isn't locked!'

'Well, that's what you expected, isn't it?' Connie pushed Cosmos along ahead of her; they might as well get this over.

'Yeah, but —' The door was ajar. It was one thing to think that something might have happened; it was quite another thing to have it proved.

He pulled tentatively on the knob and the door swung open. Behind it, the inner barred doors seemed to be in place. Locked. So that was okay. Maybe the guard had just been talking to the prisoners and hadn't bothered to lock the outer door when he — When he *what*?

Pesky glanced around uneasily. The guy had probably gone for a leak, that's all. Probably be back any minute. Cosmo and Connie were comfortably close now, just a couple of steps away. It was time to reassert his authority. He stepped forward to the barred door.

'All right, you in there,' he called to the unresponsive figure motionless at the far end of the cell. 'Don't sulk in a corner when you've got visitors. Stand up and — oh, Christ!'

'What is it? What's the —?'

'Don't look!' Pesky pushed Connie away. 'His throat —!' He began retching and staggered back from the door.

'Poor little guy.' Against his better judgement, Cosmo took Pesky's place peering through the bars. 'He wasn't so bad. Who says it's so great to spend your life sober all the time? He probably had reasons —'

Cosmo broke off, his guilty feeling at having been one of the people responsible for locking away D-and-D disappeared. They hadn't been responsible for setting him up for a killer, after all. The body in the cell wasn't D-and-D — it was Edgar, the dining-room steward.

'Don't look!' He echoed Pesky as Connie tried to slip past him. He caught her and whirled her around facing back into the corridor. He made the mistake of looking again himself. That was when he noticed the second body curled under the bunk in the other cell. The guard.

Cosmo sprang away from the bars and slammed the outer door on the scene, as though he could wipe out the fact by closing it out of sight. He leaned against the door and tried not to join Pesky in a retching match.

'What *is* it?' Connie demanded.

'Edgar . . . throat cut.' He had to answer her or she'd try to look for herself and he hadn't the strength to stop her. 'And the guard . . . head beaten in.' He drew a long shuddering breath and closed his eyes. The vision remained; he might have to live with it for the rest of his life. Of course, the way things were going aboard this ship, that might not be for very much longer.

'Mr Smithers?' Connie asked.

'No sign of him . . .' Cosmo tried to pull himself together. 'Not in there . . .'

'I told you,' Pesky said. 'I told you! He's got loose and everybody's in danger again. Look at the cold-blooded way he's killed those two people in there.'

'We'll have to tell someone,' Cosmo said feebly. 'Report it. The Captain ought to know and the others . . .'

'That's right, what about the others?' Pesky snapped to attention. 'The girls! If he's killed Edgar, maybe he's killed the girls, too. Let's go and check!' He turned and started down the corridor.

'But what would he do a thing like that for?' Connie pulled Cosmo along. 'What did they ever do to him?'

'Maybe they were all in it together,' Pesky said wildly. 'Maybe they know too much. Maybe he figures if he gets rid of them, he can get away with it. There'll be nobody to testify against him. He can say he's innocent — and there'll be nobody left to prove he isn't.'

'I don't believe it,' Connie said. 'He's not the type!'

'Hah!' Pesky said. 'In fact, ha-ha-ha-ha-ha!' His laugh was erratic and hysterical. 'Who do you think you are, Central Casting? So go ahead, tell me who *is* the type?'

'Do you know where we're going?' Cosmo tried to deflect the argument before it grew acrimonious.

'Sure I do!' Pesky snapped. 'The girls are locked in their cabin on D Deck. We're going to make sure they're still there.'

They took the lift, as much because they did not want to meet any of the passengers as for speed. Pesky threw the concealed switch that cut off any other calls. This was a direct run.

'There's no guard down there.' Connie leaned out of the lift timidly and surveyed the corridor, reluctant to leave the safety of the small enclosure.

'They didn't leave a guard on the girls,' Cosmo said. 'Edgar was the dangerous one — they thought.'

'They'll find out,' Pesky said darkly. 'I warned them that drunk act was a perfect cover, but they didn't believe me.'

'He *did* drink everything he ordered,' Connie said. 'I've watched him. I don't see how he could drink all he does and still be able to work out and carry through a plan like this.'

'Grow up! You've seen enough stage tricks. He's probably using the old funnel underneath his collar with the tube that runs down to the flask inside his belt. It's easy enough to fake.' But Pesky too hovered in the doorway, preventing the automatic doors from closing. He wasn't so anxious to walk down that corridor and knock at the cabin door, either.

'We can't stand here and argue all night.' Cosmo glanced at

his watch. 'Connie and I have a show in the Night Club in half an hour.'

'Yeah . . . well . . .' Pesky took a deep breath and moved forward. 'Let's go, folks!'

With an intense sense of *déjà vu*, Connie and Cosmo followed him reluctantly down the deserted corridor. He stopped at the door and waited until they caught up with him before he knocked.

There was no answer.

'At least the door is closed,' Connie said hopefully.

'But is it locked?' Pesky turned the knob and pushed tentatively. The door swung inwards. 'I guess not.' He stood there. He didn't want to look. He didn't have to look. The fact that the door was unlocked told everything.

The door swung open all the way. They could see the motionless bodies lying on the twin beds. Asleep?

'Hey, girls —' Pesky stepped over the threshold. 'Are you all right? . . . No —' He could see the small neat hole in the centre of each forehead now. Very small, but very deadly.

'No . . .' He stepped backward. 'No, you're not, are you? You're dead, too . . .'

'Listen, honey —' Madge Morton grabbed Mrs Anson-Pryce's arm and pulled her into a corner. 'I don't know what the hell you think about it, but I'll tell you this — over my dead body do they get my hard-earned diamonds!'

'That's the problem, isn't it?' Mrs Anson-Pryce responded coldly. 'Our dead bodies seem to be precisely what someone has in mind.'

'I mean, if you think it was a barrel of laughs living with the late Mr Morton, you can think again! All that kept me going sometimes was remembering that he had a bad heart and drove like a maniac. I tell you, I *earned* my diamonds and I'm not giving them away for anything.'

'I had a happy marriage myself,' Mrs Anson-Pryce murmured. Her diamonds were not trophies, nevertheless they had a sentimental value over and above their commercial value, which was considerable.

'So you were one of the lucky ones. Does that mean you're going to toss your diamonds into the pot with a merry laugh?'

'I wouldn't speak quite so loudly,' Mrs Anson-Pryce said quietly. 'You don't know who might be listening.'

'I don't care!' Madge glanced around defiantly. 'I'll say it to anyone.'

'That wouldn't be wise.'

'I don't care —' But Madge lowered her voice. '*Are* you?' she almost whispered. 'Are you going to let them get away with it?'

'I'm not sure what you think we can do about it.' Mrs Anson-Pryce surveyed her shipmate with distaste.

'I know what I'm going to do! I'm going to put everything into my safe in the Purser's Office and lock it up. Jewellery, money, travellers cheques even. They won't be able to get it there — it's like a Swiss bank account. Unreachable.'

'It's a thought.' Mrs Anson-Pryce carefully refrained from giving her opinion of the thought.

'Take my advice, dearie —' Madge patted her hand; Mrs Anson-Pryce drew back. 'You do the same. And the sooner, the better. Before everybody else thinks of it and there's a rush on the Purser's Office.'

'You go ahead,' Mrs Anson-Pryce said. 'I must go to my stateroom first.'

'That's right,' Madge called after her. 'Collect everything. But hurry!'

Without haste, Mrs Anson-Pryce made her way to her quarters. She had no intention of doing anything Madge had advised. Silly woman! It was obviously far too late for any of her ideas. The only chance would have been if one had never worn any of one's jewellery while on board. Only a fool could think that pirates had moved among them and not noted every gem. It was too late to attempt to hide one's wealth. Thank heavens her insurance was up to date.

She was inserting her key in the lock of her door when she heard the first faint groan. She froze.

Another groan . . . then a whimper. Coming from one of the empty staterooms. It was either a trap or someone needed help. She was not heartless. Neither was she foolhardy.

Mrs Anson-Pryce entered her own stateroom and bolted the door behind her. She lifted her telephone and called the Purser's Office, speaking briefly to the anxious voice on the other end.

'It sounded like a woman,' she concluded. 'I'm going in there now to see if I can help. Please come as quickly as you can.' She hung up on the protests and the orders to stay where she was.

She opened the door and listened. The voice had grown weaker; she could barely hear the whimper.

'Hang on,' she called. 'I'm coming.' She closed her door and bolted it again. Then she crossed to her dressing-table. She was not a fool and there was one more thing she was going to do before she ventured into the unknown.

Mrs Anson-Pryce loaded her revolver.

CHAPTER 15

'*Forty-five minutes from Broadway . . .*' Cosmo and Connie harmonized wistfully.

A muted sigh rustled through their audience. They were not the only ones who wished themselves within commuting distance of the Big Apple tonight. The night club was crowded with passengers huddled together for protection rather than entertainment.

'*. . . and, oh!, what a difference it makes . . .*'

Broadway wasn't what it used to be when that song was written. Probably New Rochelle — the town the song paid tribute to — wasn't either. But any place had to be better than the *Empress Josephine*. Give us the Great White Way — muggers, druggers, and all.

As if things weren't bad enough already, they had now alienated Pesky. He had stamped off in a rage, refusing to have anything more to do with them. And all because of one innocent little remark. Well, it would have been innocent if circumstances had been different.

'Boy —' Cosmo had said thoughtlessly — 'you sure do know where the bodies are buried!'

'What the hell are you insinuating?' Pesky had snarled.

'Nothing,' Connie had said quickly. 'Cosmo's just being silly. I mean, the bodies aren't even buried. I guess what he meant was, you sure do know where to *find* the bodies —' Too late, she had realized that that wasn't the right thing to say, either.

'So that's what you're both thinking!' Pesky had gone pale with fury. 'My friends! My pals! My buddies! You think *I'm* the killer!'

'Of course we don't,' Connie had said staunchly. But now that the idea was out in the open, they couldn't help considering it. Pesky *had* discovered a lot of bodies. Was he just unlucky or was it due to prior knowledge?

'The hell you don't!' Pesky raged. They could not blame him, not if he were innocent. Neither could they meet his eyes. They had started out by humouring him — but every wild theory had turned out to be correct. Was it just inspired guesswork — or something worse?

'Take it easy, Pesky.' Cosmo tried to close the widening rift. 'You're upset. I don't blame you. It's been a terrible experience. We don't think — not really — that you had anything to do with it. Let's pull ourselves together and go and report to the Captain. He's got to know about this.'

'We can't —' Connie nudged him. It was a long way to the Captain's quarters, through too many deserted corridors — and that empty lift. 'It's time for our show. We're due in the night club now.'

'That's right —' Pesky had unerringly picked up the thought behind the excuse. 'You run off and leave me! You don't want to be alone with me —' He bared his teeth. 'Maybe you're right.

Maybe you're next on my list! Maybe I'm going to —' He took a step forward.

Connie squealed with alarm and took refuge behind Cosmo.

'Listen, Pesky, we're sorry.' Cosmo shifted to protect Connie. 'It's true, though. You know we have to go on for the late show. Why don't you see the Captain yourself and meet us after the show for a drink?'

'Forget it!' Pesky turned away. 'Just do me one last favour, that's all. Don't call me — and I won't call you!'

Cosmo segued into another tune. This was nostalgia night — and they all knew what they were nostalgic for.

'*Give my regards to Broadway . . .*' Never mind that it was probably below zero, hip-deep in piled-up snow and with more blizzards on the way. It would be bliss to be there tonight.

'*Remember me to Herald Square . . .*'

'All right, take it easy.' Dr Parker's gentle fingers probed the base of Joan's skull, delicately measuring the length and breadth of the contusion, assessing the probable damage. 'You're going to be all right. You'll have a nasty headache for a while, though.'

'What happened?' Mrs Anson-Pryce asked. Having discovered and reported the latest victim, she was taking a proprietary interest in the proceedings. No one quite dared to order her back to her stateroom.

'I was going about my duties —' Joan tried to sit up, but had to give up and lie back. Carl Daniels was looking gratifyingly worried. 'I'd just turned down Mrs Anson-Pryce's bed and was leaving the cabin when I thought I saw someone going into one of the unoccupied cabins. I followed to investigate and — and that's all I can remember.'

'That was a very silly thing to do,' Mrs Anson-Pryce scolded. 'You should have called for someone to go with you.'

'It didn't occur to me,' Joan said. She frowned. 'I didn't think I needed to,' she amended. 'From the glimpse I caught, I thought it was one of the crew. One of the officers . . .'

'Who?' Carl Daniels clenched his fists and looked ready to do instant battle.

'I don't know. I only saw him disappearing into the cabin. I got the impression of a uniform. It needn't have been so. It might have been one of the passengers in Fancy —' She stopped, remembering that she had watched the contestants assembling outside the Main Lounge. No one had been wearing anything that resembled an officer's uniform.

'You must think. Concentrate, my dear. It's very important.' Mrs Anson-Pryce spoke as though she were the only one to realize this. But the thought was in all their minds. The killer had slipped up again. For the second time, an intended victim had been left alive; this time, a possible witness.

'She may remember a bit more after she's had a rest,' Dr Parker said quickly. 'Or,' he added cheerfully, 'it may be a blank for the rest of her life.'

The others looked at him suspiciously; he was entirely too cheerful about that possibility.

'But there's nothing to remember,' Joan protested. 'The cabin was dark, I couldn't see a thing. I went to turn on the light and then —' she grimaced ruefully — 'I saw stars.'

'You're sure?' Mrs Anson-Pryce was disappointed.

'Certain . . .' Joan's voice belied the word. Something was niggling at the edge of her consciousness. *Had* there been something too familiar about the figure she had seen? Was it that she honestly could not remember anything — or that, down deep, she didn't want to? She shuddered.

'That's enough,' Dr Parker said firmly. 'It's off to your bunk now and get some sleep. For you, the night is over.'

For others, it was just beginning. Captain Falcon gave brusque orders for the newly-discovered bodies to be carried down to what had once been the hospital, but was now the morgue. He detailed search-parties to hunt for missing passenger D. D. Smithers — if he were still to be found. The deep dark sea was all around them and there was no guarantee that he had not been thrown overboard after his release from the brig. If he was innocent, he might have been released for that very purpose. So that the crew would concentrate their efforts on trying to find him, under the assumption that he was the killer, while the real killer had already disposed of him and was going about his deadly business unsuspected.

'What's the toll?' Captain Falcon demanded grimly.

'Sir?' It had been a long watch, the other officers were momentarily confused.

'The toll for today and tonight? How many has he accounted for — so far?'

'Edgar . . .' Carl Daniels began counting up. 'The two girls . . . possibly Smithers . . . the guard may not survive . . .'

'One passenger had a heart attack,' Dr Parker put in. 'But that was a natural death. On the other hand, on a less stressful voyage, it might not have happened. I don't know how you'd count it.'

'It's not how we'd count it,' Captain Falcon said. 'It's how the killer counts that concerns me.'

'He tried for Joan,' Daniels said, 'but he didn't succeed. Of course, that was in a main passenger area and he didn't have much time. As it was, Mrs Anson-Pryce must have nearly caught him.'

'That makes . . .' Captain Falcon added up the names . . . 'four definite deaths, two possible and one attempt. Six, if we count them all. And this was the seventh day. According to the killer's schedule, there's one more to go. Two, if he doesn't count the heart attack.'

'I think we should put it about that we consider the killer directly responsible for the heart attack,' Parker said. 'I'm sure Mrs Baldwin will go along. It might save another death. I feel the killer isn't so much interested in actually murdering passengers as for getting the credit for it. After all, he never went back to finish off Smithers after he missed him with the poisoned water —'

'Unless he's caught up with the poor devil now,' Daniels said.

'Or unless Smithers is the killer!' Pesky could keep quiet no longer. 'I tell you, he's the one! I swear it!'

The look that Captain Falcon directed at him reminded him that, in olden days, they had slain the bearer of bad news. It had been bad enough to report the deaths of Edgar and the croupiers; he was really crowding his luck by arguing now.

'Either that, or we've got a stowaway on board,' Pesky hedged quickly.

'Impossible!' Captain Falcon snapped back. 'With the number of times this ship has been searched, we'd have found any unauthorized personnel by this time.'

'Okay —' Pesky no longer cared. 'In that case, it's either D-and-D or one of your own officers! Take your pick!'

Captain Falcon lurched to his feet. 'Throw that man in irons!' he bellowed in automatic reflex.

'Equity!' Pesky babbled. 'American Guild of Variety Artists! You can't do that to me. I've got connections —' He cast about wildly. 'ASCAP! Theatre Guild! We've got rules — laws! Equity won't let you do this to me! Equity —' he bleated. 'Equity — where are you?'

'Steady on, Calhoun.' Fingers like iron bands fastened themselves around Pesky's forearm and pulled him towards the door. 'Just come along quietly —' The voice dropped. 'We'll sort this out later. Just don't antagonize the Captain any more. He has enough problems to contend with.'

'He has!' Pesky gave a wild laugh, but allowed the Purser to ease him through the door.

'Please, Pesky —' Daniels was not aware of the thin edge of desperation in his own voice. 'Just shut up and go to your cabin. Get some sleep. There's nothing more you can do tonight — but we're going to need you in the morning to help us keep control. Once the passengers have had a chance to think things over, they're going to be on the verge of panic. Tomorrow's going to be a hell of a day!'

'They've all been hells of days!' Pesky said fervently. 'It's

about time the pasengers shared some of the load. Why should
we take all the strain?'

'Because it's our job.' Daniels propelled him towards the
stairs. 'The passengers have paid their fares and they have a
right to expect a smooth passage. It's up to us to see that they get
it. In your world, they call it "the show must go on."'

'Yeah —?' Pesky balked at the head of the stairs. 'Let me tell
you, chum, even in *my* world, we ring down the curtain when
somebody yells *"Fire!"* That's when we put up the house lights
and start directing the audience to the nearest exits.'

'I wish we could, Pesky,' Daniels said sombrely. 'But we
don't have any exits. There's nowhere for them to go — except
Davy Jones's Locker.'

Nothing, the search-parties reported back. Nothing in the cargo
hold; nothing in the unoccupied cabins; nothing in any of the
possible hiding-places; nothing in the impossible places. *Nothing
and no one.*

Nevertheless, the search-parties would continue to patrol the
ship all night.

Daniels nodded curtly, acknowledging the last of the reports.
He had set up a table and chair blocking the door to Joan's cabin
and was receiving reports there. To hell with the raised eyebrows and smirks — he would trust no one else to guard her door.
There had been a guard on the brig — and look what happened.

The lights were low, muted chimes could be heard signalling
the next watch. The dog watch. The hours when life dropped to
its lowest ebb and could slip away on the tide. Resistance was
lowered, defences were down; the low throb of the engines was
hypnotic; the soft roll of the ship soporific. Daniels leaned back
in his chair and felt his eyes closing.

Almost asleep, he became aware of approaching footsteps.
Abruptly Daniels remembered that the killer had one more
victim to despatch before he had accomplished his self-
appointed mission for the day. Had he decided to finish off Joan
and perhaps take care of her guard at the same time? He had

been specializing in guards and their charges today. And this was how it had been done: a bored guard — exhausted, in his case — falling asleep on duty and easily approached.

Daniels tensed. He opened his eyes to slits and turned his head, as though it were rolling in sleep, in the direction of the footsteps. But the sounds had ceased.

'Good evening, Mr Daniels,' a voice said from the other side of him. He jumped.

'I'm sorry I startled you,' Mrs Anson-Pryce said. 'I thought I'd come by and see how the stewardess was recovering from her ordeal.' Her voice shaded into reproof. '*I'm* not able to sleep after all that.'

'I've had a few other things to do, as well.' Damned if he would apologize. Why should he? Come to that, why should he believe what she had just said? It was a good excuse for prowling around where she had no right to be. He looked at her with sudden suspicion. There was no guarantee that the pirate had to be a man. The old lady was tough. She had obviously led a long hard life. She might be capable of anything.

'Of course.' She forgave him graciously. 'But if you're so tired, is it wise for you to try to guard the door? You'd be much better off getting a good night's sleep and letting someone else do guard duty . . .' She hesitated, perhaps becoming aware of his suspicious gaze.

'I'm all right.' His gaze moved to the handbag weighing down her arm. A memory stirred. On the first search of the ship, Joan had reported that Mrs Anson-Pryce was in possession of a pearl-handled revolver. It looked as though she was carrying it now.

'As I said,' Mrs Anson-Pryce persisted, 'I'm quite unable to sleep. I would be most willing to take your place until morning. I assure you —' she patted her handbag — 'I'm quite able to protect her.'

'I'm sure you are.' Daniels gave her a brief unenthusiastic smile. The girl croupiers had been shot. 'But it's my job. We can't have the passengers taking over our jobs. Seamen's Union would object.'

'Nevertheless —' she was unsmiling — 'you're not fit to carry out your duties right now. You need help; I am willing to provide it.'

'That's very kind of you, Mrs Anson-Pryce, but I'm afraid I must decline your kind offer. I was a bit sleepy when you approached, but I'm quite alert now — and I intend to remain so.'

'In other words —' she was not a fool — 'you don't trust me.'

'Let's just say that I don't trust anyone right now.'

'In that case, you will not be surprised to learn that *I* do not trust *you*.' She raised a hand to silence a protest he did not intend to make. 'The fact that you are a ship's officer cuts little ice with me in this situation. It must be apparent to the meanest intelligence that these atrocious murders could only have been carried out by someone thoroughly familiar with the ship's routine. A deeper familiarity than mere passengers could acquire. I believe we must look to the crew — and I would not rule out the officers.'

'I promise you, I'm ruling out no one,' Daniels said. 'That's why I'm standing guard myself.'

'In that case,' she looked at him with cold mistrust, 'you won't object if I join you.'

'As you please.' He inclined his head, determined that he would not stand and give her his chair. If she wanted to stand guard, then stand would be the word. He had no fear of nodding off again — not with her there.

'I *do* please.' She folded her arms and leaned against the wall opposite. 'I can understand how it could happen, you know. Sailors must resent spending their time catering to the whims of a lot of people they consider silly and useless. It must have been a great temptation to relieve us of our money and jewellery, to make one great swoop and disappear with the spoils thinking to live in luxury for the rest of one's days. In a way, one could almost sympathize — if it were not for all the wanton killing.'

'On the other hand,' Daniels said evenly, 'I can easily understand how it might have been a passenger. One who's done a lot of cruising — most ships follow the same routine. Perhaps someone on a fixed income eroded by inflation or illness, or facing bankruptcy because of bad investments might succumb to the temptation. Someone elderly, who might figure they hadn't all that much to lose and would prefer not to live through the sunset years at all, rather than have to live through them in penury. Someone like that might not care about risking their own life, so why should they worry about wasting a few other lives? Yes, it could very well be one of the passengers.'

They faced each other implacably. In silence, the dislike and distrust rankling between them, they prepared to wait out the remainder of the night.

Captain Falcon and First Mate Hanson stared incredulously at the interloper, unable to believe they had heard what they had just heard. Captain Falcon was the first to recover.

'See here, mister,' he snapped, 'I don't care if you *are* one of the VIP passengers. No one tells me how to run my ship!'

'Forgive me,' Herr Otto von Schreiber said, 'I have not made myself clear. This is not your ship, Captain Falcon, it is mine.'

'You mean you're —?' Captain Falcon reached for the weapon in his desk drawer, cursing himself inwardly for not having it ready to hand. He could be killed before he got it half way out of the drawer. Unless, of course, they needed him alive.

'*Gott in Himmel!*' von Schreiber exploded. 'You *still* do not understand. I say this is my ship and I mean it. All the ships of this Line are mine. I am the owner of the Line!'

'The owner? On board?' Captain Falcon glared about him, at everyone and no one. 'Why wasn't I told?'

'It was not customary courtesy, true. For that, I apologize. But one must travel incognito at times. How else can one determine that all is as it should be? A crew forewarned is a crew on its best behaviour. I wish to observe the normal behaviour so that I may be certain that passengers are properly treated.'

'You don't need to worry about that.' Captain Falcon was
indignant. 'Not on board the *Empress Josephine*. This ship is the
finest —'

'*Ja, ja* —' von Schreiber interrupted warily. 'But not, I think,
on this voyage.'

'No.' Captain Falcon accepted the correction. 'These circumstances are exceptional.'

'They are abominable! That is what I have said. They must
not be allowed to continue. The safety of the passengers must be
paramount!'

'We're doing everything we can. And the safety of the passengers *is* paramount.'

'Then why have so many died?'

'Because we're not mind-readers! Because the devils struck
without warning. Because they deliberately killed without giving us a chance to fight them — or even buy them off. Because
we didn't know what was happening until it was too late to save
some of the passengers.'

'*Ja, so*. Now that we know, we must save the rest. Even
though —' von Schreiber sighed — 'we must submit to black-
mail to do so. First, we must save the lives. Then we can
concentrate on revenge. I will post such rewards that the ends of
the earth will not be safe for these demons.'

'My sentiments exactly,' Captain Falcon agreed. 'I'm not
sure, though, that all the passengers will be willing to pay up.'

'They have nothing to fear. The Line will reimburse them.'

'I wouldn't announce that until it's all over. The pirates
might try for more if they thought there was more available.'

'*Ja*, you are right. We must not complicate things at this
point. We must give them what they want and see that they get
clear of the ship before we do anything else. You must, of course,
take every precaution to ensure that they do not sabotage the
Empress Josephine before they leave her.'

'We'd thought of that,' Captain Falcon said coldly. 'From
now until the ship docks in Nhumbala, there will be a twenty-
four-hour guard on all vital points.'

'You are docking, then, at Nhumbala? Rumour has said that the capital has been seized by rebel forces.'

'Maybe it has — and maybe it hasn't. The Government were fighting back. They've had a chance to win by this time. Our radio was wrecked and we won't know who's in control until we get there. But we'll do better to take our chances there, rather than risk sailing another couple of days to get to a different port.' Ironically, the contraband cargo they had been duped into carrying would ensure their welcome no matter which side was in control. However, it might be best not to admit that to the Owner of the Line. With a bit of luck, that was something Herr von Schreiber need never know.

'I won't feel comfortable,' Captain Falcon said truthfully, 'until we've disembarked all the passengers. What happens to them after that is their own responsibility.'

'Perhaps you are right.' Von Schreiber nodded. 'They will not be in any more danger on land than aboard ship, certainly. A foe who can be faced can be reasoned with. These others, they are moving fast now. They must. We are due to dock in three more days.'

'We're moving fast ourselves,' Captain Falcon said grimly. 'We'll be docking sooner than that. We've gained thirty hours on our schedule already.'

'*Ja*, I had thought we were moving at greater speed. It is possible that the pirates also have noticed it. If so, they may be forced into moving more quickly than they intended.'

'I'd say it must be just about time for another communication from them. The next move is up to them.'

CHAPTER 16

Connie opened her eyes and couldn't close them again. A thin streak of daylight showed between the curtains over the port-hole. It was morning and it was all too much to face. She closed her eyes, but they popped open immediately. The cabin was full of shadows made more sinister by the streak of light.

It was silly. Of course she was safe in here with Cosmo beside her. No one could have sneaked in here while they were asleep. Not possibly. Not without a key. The bedroom steward held a master key. Was that a movement in the corner? The bathroom door swinging open — because the latch had not caught? Or because someone —?

'Cosmo —' She rolled over and jabbed a forefinger into his ribs. 'Cosmo, it's morning.'

'Yes, I'd noticed.' He did not open his eyes. 'I was trying to ignore it.'

The bathroom door swung to and closed with a little snick. They'd noticed the latch was defective the first night aboard, now that she came to think about it. Now that Cosmo was awake and she could think clearly again.

'Well, aren't you going to get up?'

'Give me three good reasons why.' His eyes remained obstinately closed. 'Give me one.'

'Time —' She squinted at her watch in the crack of daylight. 'Time to take the joggers out. Pesky will be expecting . . .' She trailed off. She had forgotten. That was no longer a good reason.

'Pesky will not be expecting me.' Cosmo corrected her. 'Pesky will cut me dead — if he doesn't punch my head off. He might do both.'

'He'll have cooled off by now,' she said unconvincingly. 'He'll feel better after a good night's sleep.'

'Do you?'

'Of course not. Oh, Cosmo!' She hurled herself into his arms. 'It's all my fault. If I hadn't wanted to be working too, we could still be in Florida. I could have lazed on the beach while you were rehearsing at the Playhouse and I could have sold tickets in the evenings to help out at performances.'

'It's not your fault,' he comforted her. 'It was a joint decision and it was right. You're too good to waste on a beach. Look at all we've learned working together here. We'll be the new Lunt and Fontanne.'

'If we survive.' Her voice was muffled.

'We've got to survive.' Cosmo dropped into a wicked imitation of Pesky. 'Think of the loss to the American theatre if we don't. It's our duty to survive.'

'You're right.' Connie did her own imitation of Pesky. 'We owe it to future generations of theatre-goers!'

They clung together and began to laugh. Suddenly Connie's laughter turned to tears. It wasn't funny. It was true.

Daniels opened his eyes and looked straight into a pair of staring eyes directly across from him. For a terrible moment, he thought she was dead, that the killer had stalked the corridor while he'd slept and . . .

'Good morning, Mr Daniels,' she said.

'Good morning, Mrs Anson-Pryce,' he responded coldly. There was no point in pretending he hadn't been asleep. She had him dead to rights. Rather, she hadn't had him dead, so perhaps she was innocent of the crimes levelled against her by his suspicious mind. Unfortunately that did not make him like her any the better.

'I trust you slept well.' She was not improving the situation. 'You did need to sleep. It's as well I was here.'

The door opened behind him. Joan stood there, in uniform, ready to start another day. She stared down at Daniels, blocking her doorway. 'What on earth —?'

'Good morning —' He lurched to his feet, pushing the small table to one side.

'Good morning, my dear,' Mrs Anson-Pryce said. 'Are you feeling better?'

'Still a bit sore and aching. I'll ask Dr Parker for a couple more tablets, then I'll be quite all right.'

'Oh, do you think you should? I feel it's always best to fight these things yourself. It's so unwise to depend on tablets.'

The words were unexceptional, but the tone was wrong. Joan

and Carl exchanged glances. Mrs Anson-Pryce didn't trust Dr Parker, either.

The breakfast chimes for first sitting rippled along the corridor. Moving swiftly, Mrs Anson-Pryce pushed herself away from the wall. 'I shall go to my stateroom and freshen up,' she announced. 'If at any time, my dear —' she looked at Joan — 'you need any help or advice, feel free to call on me.' She turned slowly and, moving stiffly but with magnficent dignity, left them.

'Good heavens,' Joan said. 'What was that all about? What are you doing here, anyway? Both of you?' They followed Mrs Anson-Pryce into the passenger section.

'We were on guard duty. She doesn't trust me.' Carl's lips quirked wryly. 'Perhaps she's got a point. You were pretty certain the man who attacked you was wearing an officer's uniform. You seem to have convinced her.'

'Oh, really!' Joan flushed. 'I wish —' She did not continue. Cabin doors were opening and passengers were crowding into the corridor on their way to first sitting.

All except one of them. Madge Morton bore down on them. 'Mr Daniels, I've been looking for you. I'm sorry, I know the Purser's Office isn't open yet. Officially. But this is very urgent —' She had reached them now and lowered her voice, glancing around suspiciously.

'I must add something to my safe-deposit box. Don't tell me it can't be done. The way things are going on this ship, there aren't any rules any more. It's your job to help us save all we can — and this is too valuable to throw to a load of thieves. So you just come along this instant and open up the Purser's Office for me!'

'Yes, ma'am.' No use arguing. There was just one problem: the thieves were unlikely to overlook the rich spoils on deposit in the Purser's Office. When the crunch came, did she imagine that he would risk having more hostages killed by refusing to hand over the contents of the safes?

The corridor had emptied as rapidly as it had filled. Joan

walked as far as the lobby with them, then slipped away while
Carl unlocked the Purser's Office. He tried, unsuccessfully, to
block Madge Morton from following him in, but she pushed
past him.

He had nearly reached the bank of safe-deposit boxes when
he heard the door shut and the lock click. He halted. ·

The shutters were down. No one in the lobby could see into
the Office. Momentarily he hoped that she might have stepped
outside and locked him in alone. Then he heard the soft footfall
behind him and knew that she was still there. One of the
passengers . . . one of the pirates?

'Hurry up,' she said. 'No one saw us come in except the
stewardess — and she won't talk. If we hurry, we can get it over
with and be out again with no one the wiser. Box Twenty-four.
Here's my key.'

Daniels took a deep breath and accepted the key. Box 24. He
found his own master key. She rummaged in her handbag and
produced a rolled padded silk jewel case.

Daniels opened the safe and pulled out the box. He lifted the
hinged lid and drew out the large manilla envelope inside. Then
he froze.

'Here —' She thrust the jewel case at him. It was lumpy and
very heavy. She must have crammed everything she owned into
it.

He hoped that his face had not changed expression, betraying
him. He fumbled the envelope open, hurriedly dropped the
jewel case inside and replaced it in the box. He pushed the box
back into its niche.

'Wait a minute,' she said. 'I want to take one more look —'

'There isn't time.' He slammed the door shut; it locked
automatically. Locked — that was a laugh!

'No —' Chimes announced the second sitting. 'I guess there
isn't,' she agreed reluctantly.

He saw her to the door, unlocked it for her and looked out to
make sure the lobby was empty before he stepped back to let her
out. She sprang away from the door and turned quickly,

managing to look as though she had approached the lobby from a different direction and had never been near the Purser's Office at all.

He closed the door silently behind her, locked it and leaned against it for a moment, gathering strength before he could force himself back to the safes.

The envelope in Box 24 had been empty.

Mrs Anson-Pryce had the finest collection of jewels on board. He found the list of names and checked: she had Box 10. His hand had begun to shake. It took three stabs at the lock before the master key slid into it and turned.

His heart began to sink as he pulled out the box. Surely, it was too light. He flipped up the lid and gazed down at the flat manilla envelope. Empty.

The telephone began to ring, but he ignored it. He started methodically at the top left-hand box and worked his way down and across, opening every box with his master key.

Every box was empty.

While he had been sleeping, the pirates had struck, plundering the Purser's Office. Unseen and undetected, they had escaped with a king's ransom in gems.

A ship's ransom?

Pesky found the seventh body of the seventh day. Or was it the first body of the eighth day? He stared down at it blankly, shaking his head.

'No,' he said firmly, as though the body were arguing with him. 'No, it's just too much. I'm not going to do it.'

What the hell? Why did it always have to happen to him? No wonder everybody was looking sideways at him. If he didn't know better, he'd suspect him, too. How come he always had to find the bodies?

All he'd been going to do was just drop in and have a cheerful word with old Bert, the mechanic. See if he was having any luck repairing the radio set. See if they were back in contact with the world.

And look what he found: Bert — dead. Head bashed in. It wasn't fair. Poor Bert.

Poor Pesky. What about him? His nerves were shot to hell. He'd never dare walk into another room for fear of what he might find. This ship was ruining his health — not to mention his reputation. Even his best friends were beginning to suspect him. If he had to report another body . . .

'Sorry, Bert,' Pesky apologized. 'If you were still alive, I'd have done anything for you. But now — no way! I'm not going to do it. You just stay there, pal. The next one along will have to report it. As far as I'm concerned, I've never seen you.'

Pesky backed out of the Radio Room cautiously and closed the door on his dead shipmate.

D. D. Smithers woke and stretched. Tried to stretch. His feet encountered an obstruction; so did his arms. He tried to raise his head, but it thumped against a hard wooden board immediately above it. He saw stars, then opened his eyes and could not see anything at all.

He gave up, lay completely still and tried to work out his position. A terrible thought came to him, bringing a chill sweat in its wake.

Very carefully he put out a hand, exploring his surroundings. There was an obstruction, then a curved hollow behind it. Farther along, another obstruction, another curved hollow. There was an obstruction immediately above his head, but above that was more space, higher than he could reach. He exhaled a long sigh of relief. It was all right. He still didn't know where he was, but he was not in a coffin.

He was still aboard ship. The motion told him that. But where? In a closet? Back in the hold?

He seemed to be lying on a thin foam mattress; a blanket had wrapped itself around his legs, restricting them. He'd evidently made himself comfortable somewhere — but where?

Then his groping hand encountered something friendly and familiar in the frightening darkness. A bottle. He traced its curves: a whisky bottle. He lifted it and shook it: about half full.

Just what he needed. Nasty shock for a man, waking up like this. Could make him begin to think the DTs had caught up with him — just the way Marsha had always predicted. Enough to make him wonder if he ought to climb on that famous wagon.

Hair of the dog that bit him, that was what he needed. Then he'd remember where he was and what he was doing here. More important, how to get out of here.

Carefully he unscrewed the cap, guided the bottle to his lips and drank deeply. That was better. So much better. He still didn't remember where he was, but he didn't mind so much now. He took another drink. Yes, that was a great improvement.

He was on board the *Empress Josephine* — the unfriendliest ship he had ever seen. Furthermore, all sorts of unpleasant things were happening on board her. No matter where he was, he was well out of it for the time being.

There was no hurry at all to get back to the bunch of snobs who kept cold-shouldering him. It was rather pleasant to be out of range of the strange man who kept shouting accusations at him and banging his head against the nearest hard object.

No one would miss him. No one would come looking for him. No one would care where he was.

He heard a sound like a sob and looked around. But he already knew there was no one else here. It must have come from him. That would never do.

'Play the game, ol' boy,' he admonished himself. He took one more drink and then one more, relaxing. Must be near mealtime . . . which meal? Did it matter? . . . Not while the bottle held out.

Meanwhile, it was dark . . . night . . . time to have 'nother little sleep and worry about things in the morning.

He drank deeply, then recapped the bottle and tucked it under his arm. He wriggled into a more comfortable position. Time enough to worry about it in the morning . . .

Captain Falcon picked up the luncheon menu and bared his teeth in a savage smile he flashed around the table. He was here to show the flag, but he didn't have to like it.

'Ah, lunch . . .' Herr von Schreiber lifted his menu as though it were weighted down with lead. 'Something light, I think. A salad, perhaps.'

'A salad . . .' his wife echoed. For once, she seemed indifferent to food.

'I'm not hungry,' Hallie Ordway said flatly. She looked across at Mary Lawton and Mrs Anson-Pryce. 'Are you?'

'No —' Mary pushed away her menu unopened.

'Come, come, ladies,' Captain Falcon said with false heartiness. 'Must keep your strength up —' He groke off as their combined gaze focused on him. Damn it! It wasn't his fault, what was happening.

'Quite right, Captain Falcon.' Mrs Anson-Pryce came to his rescue. 'We must all carry on as usual . . . as long as we are able.' She took up her menu firmly, opened it — and turned pale. She let it fall back on the table.

'Are you all right?' Hallie cried anxiously. 'What's the matter? You're not going to faint, are you?'

'No —' Mrs Anson-Pryce picked up the menu again and fanned herself rapidly with it. 'No, I'm not going to faint.'

'Hhhmmmph!' Captain Falcon opened his own menu. Life was difficult enough these days without bothering about the vapours of females. He was not really hungry himself, but he had to set a good example. That was why he had come to lunch in the first place. He glanced perfunctorily at the menu — and froze.

Across the table, Herr von Schreiber cursed violently and vehemently in German. He too was staring down at his menu.

One by one they opened their menus and gazed incredulously at the printed message masking the list of entrees.

The pirates had issued their final demands.

CHAPTER 17

'Oh well,' Hallie said. 'It was fun while it lasted.' Slowly she stripped off the diamond ear-rings, the necklace, the bracelet, the rings, and dropped them into the deep plush-lined box on the table in front of Captain Falcon. He winced as each piece fell with a muted clink.

'I'm sorry, Mrs Ordway,' he said. 'I apologize deeply that this should be happening on my ship.'

She gave a short sharp laugh, then shrugged. 'Why apologize? Nobody's blaming you. Come on, Mortie —' she jerked her head at her husband — 'your turn.'

He came forward slowly, unbuttoning his diamond cuff-links. The diamond stickpin in his tie flashed as he moved.

The Ordways had chosen to wear their jewellery up to the moment of parting with it, unlike some of the other passengers who were clutching small bundles.

'Here goes nothing!' Mortimer Ordway dropped the cuff-links into the box, added the tie-pin, glanced at his watch and hesitated. 'Do you suppose they'll want this, too?' he asked Captain Falcon.

'How should I know?' Captain Falcon snarled. Did they imagine he was in cahoots with the pirates?

'Oh, don't be so damn chintzy, Mortie,' Hallie said. 'Throw it in!' She winked gallantly. 'Maybe we can get on another quiz show some day.'

'Sure, honey.' He unbuckled the watch and dropped it into the box with a sigh.

Grinding his teeth, Captain Falcon ticked off their names on the passenger list, as he had been ordered to do. He was aware that the next in line had moved up to the box. He raised his eyes and saw the von Schreibers.

Herr von Schreiber stood with thunderous face as his wife

opened her jewel box and transferred the contents to the box on the table. 'I will replace them,' he promised. 'Every one.'

'Otto, Otto —' She patted his hand 'It does not matter. We are not children that we must impress the world with our toys. When we married, we had nothing but each other. And if again we have only each other —' she smiled up at him — 'it is enough.'

A spasm of emotion crossed his face. Clicking his heels, he bowed from the waist and kissed her hand. Then he straightened, offered her his arm and led her proudly away.

But not far. There seemed to be some compulsion for the people who had already dropped their treasures into the box to stay and watch as the others gave up their belongings. The von Schreibers took their place in the front row of the solemn audience. So must primitive tribes have watched the procession leading human sacrifices to the altar.

Captain Falcon recognized Otto von Schreiber's state of controlled fury as akin to his own. And for the same reason. It was von Schreiber's ship, too. They were both shamed that such a thing could be happening aboard her; both equally determined on eventual revenge.

Mrs Anson-Pryce walked up to the box in a blaze of defiance. Like the Ordways, she had chosen to wear most of her gems up to the moment of parting. Without a word, she removed them now and slid them into the box. There was a sigh of sympathy from someone in the audience as the great diamond necklace disappeared from sight.

Captain Falcon ticked off her name and gave a silent signal to the First Mate. The box was now full. Hanson relayed the signal to the two crewmen waiting outside and they carried in another box. They removed the full box and placed it under the table, where it was to remain — with the other boxes as they filled — in plain view of everyone until instructions were received as to what to do with them.

Something in the way Madge Morton approached the box alerted Captain Falcon. He'd seen that look in the eye of a renegade deckhand once, just before the man ran amok. He watched her warily.

She carried a black velvet jewel roll and quickly dropped it into the box. There was a murmur of dissatisfaction from the watchers.

'Hey!' Hallie called out. 'She can't *do* that!'

'I'm sorry, Mrs Morton —' Captain Falcon spoke between clenched teeth. That he should be reduced to acting as spokesman for criminals! 'You know what the instructions said. You'll have to unwrap your jewellery before you put it in the box.' He reached in and took out the jewel roll — it seemed curiously light — and returned it to her.

'Oh . . . well . . .' In a swift movement, she held the roll over the box and shook it out quickly. Several small items tumbled into the box. She smiled weakly and tried to move away.

'Wait a minute —' Hallie seemed to have constituted herself spokesperson for the others. 'Where's the rest of it?'

'Oh, I'm sorry —' Madge removed a small diamond ring from her finger and added it to the box. 'There!'

'Don't hand me that! You know damn well what I mean.' Hellie moved forward and dipped her hand into the box, bringing up a small assortment of minor pieces of jewellery; the ring Madge had just tossed in was the only diamond item.

Captain Falcon winced. Even he had noticed that Madge Morton possessed more jewellery than that.

'What are you trying to pull?' Hallie demanded. 'Where are all those diamonds?'

'I . . . I haven't got them,' Madge faltered.

'What do you mean — you haven't got them? You'd better get them. You know what the instructions said — anybody who holds out is putting the rest of us in danger. Where are they?'

'Well, if you must know —' Madge faced her defiantly; the discordant rumblings in the background were making it clear that Hallie had more support than she had.

'If you must know, I put them all in my safe-deposit box in the

Purser's Office this morning. And I can't get them back because then I threw my key overboard. So there!'

'You stupid crazy bitch!' Hallie raged. 'That's just the kind of smartass trick that could get us all killed!'

'Please, ladies, please —' Captain Falcon intervened, afraid that he might have to separate them physically in a moment. It was bad enough as things were, without having a cat fight on his hands. 'This is just delaying the proceedings. Just move along —' he gave Madge a menacing frown — 'and we'll sort this out later.'

Madge pushed Hallie and hesitated. One look at the hostile faces confronting her changed whatever plan she might have had for joining the others. She tossed her head and left the Main Lounge quickly.

'All right —' Captain Falcon called attention back to the matter in hand. 'Next, please . . .'

'Who was that?' Joan had been watching the long sad procession of passengers filing into the Main Lounge to hand over their valuables, so very different from the high-spirited line-up for the Fancy Dress Ball last night. Out of the corner of her eye she had caught a glimpse of white disappearing around a corner; yet most of the officers were either standing by in the Lounge or on guard at the entrances and exits. Had one of the Duty Officers from the Bridge slipped down to take a peek at the proceedings?

'Who? I didn't see anyone.' Pesky turned round carefully, also managing to avoid seeing Connie and Cosmo who were standing near by.

'Oh, never mind.' Joan shrugged away the nagging feeling that there was something terribly familiar about the shadowy figure — and the way it had melted away. Could it have been the person who had attacked her? She shivered and moved slightly closer to Pesky. He wasn't much protection, but he might be some. She wished that he would stop sulking and close ranks with Connie and Cosmo. Safety in numbers.

More and more passengers crowded into the Lounge, as

though playing a giant game of 'Sardines'. Few of them came out again. Perhaps they, too, felt there was safety in numbers.

Only Madge Morton had been seen to leave — and that was scarcely surprising. With the trick she had pulled and the consequent enmity she had engendered, she would do well to lock herself in her cabin for the remainder of the voyage.

'Listen, Joan —' Pesky nudged her sharply.

'What?' She drew back, rubbing her bruised ribcage, and looked at him without favour.

'You're sure it wasn't D-and-D you saw? He's around here somewhere. He's got to be. He couldn't just vanish off the face of the earth — the ship.'

'He could,' she said coldly, 'if he went over the side.'

'Naw! I don't believe that. It's too easy. It's what he wants us to believe. He's out there somewhere . . . laughing at us —' Pesky broke off as he noticed her expression. 'You're just like the rest of them. You think I'm crazy, don't you?'

'Not crazy, no.' She edged away from him. 'Just perhaps a little . . . obsessed.'

'All right!' Pesky snarled. 'I've got the message.' He turned and flounced away. 'Forget it!' he hurled back over his shoulder. 'Forget the whole thing — and when you're murdered in your beds, don't come to me for sympathy!' He turned the corner and his voice faded, still grumbling.

Joan, Connie and Cosmo exchanged brief commiserative glances.

'*AAaaargh!* . . . No! . . . No! . . .' The anguished scream snapped them to attention and sent them running down the corridor after Pesky.

'Oh God . . . *no!*' Pesky reeled back into sight, trying to fend off a woman who was clutching at him. clinging to him, even as her strength gave way and she slid down his body to the floor.

'Not another!' He cringed against the wall, staring down unbelievingly at the body at his feet. 'No! I can't take any more! No —!' He made feeble flapping motions at the still form, as though trying to shoo her away.

'No-o-o . . .' His voice had risen hysterically, echoing down the corridor. Heads began to turn just inside the doors of the Main Lounge. A few passengers straggled out into the corridor and followed Joan and the Carpenters as they rushed towards Pesky.

'It can't be true —' Pesky looked at them pleadingly as they came up to him. 'Not me! Not again! I'm hallucinating. Make her go away!'

Madge Morton lay face down, a knife hilt protruding between her shoulder-blades. The knife pinned a piece of paper to her body. Rivulets of blood ran down the stark white paper, but the hand-printed message could still be read clearly:

'PREPARE TO LAUNCH NO. 1 LIFEBOAT.'

They had received the awaited ultimatum.

'Let's face it,' Hallie said. 'That broad had it coming.'

Mrs Anson-Pryce was forced to agree. She had seldom encountered a more tiresome woman, silly and selfish, and dangerously stupid to antagonize a known killer. What use were Madge Morton's precious diamonds to her now?

'We're lucky it was only her that got it,' Hallie went on darkly. 'She might have got him so mad he decided to polish off the whole day's quota before he leaves the ship.'

They were at the Lifeboat Station on the Promenade Deck watching the preparations for launching No. 1 lifeboat. The immediate area had been roped off and the curious were congregated on the other side of the rope.

'I don't believe he'll kill any more now,' Mrs Anson-Pryce said. 'He's got what he wants.'

'I sure hope so.' Hallie looked over her shoulder nervously. 'He's nobody you want to fool around with.'

More than a few passengers were of that opinion. They had gone below and locked themselves in their cabins as soon as the gathering in the Main Lounge had begun to disperse. The sight

of Madge Morton's body, carried past them this time without
any attempt at concealment, had been the last straw for many of
them. An óbject lesson in what might happen if you made
yourself conspicuous; they were going to keep out of sight until it
was all over.

A door opened leading into the cleared area and several
officers emerged carrying the boxes so recently filled with booty.
They stacked the boxes along the rail, just beside the place
where a hinged section would be swung back to provide a
gateway to the lifeboat.

'There goes my little all,' Hallie murmured, eyes fixed on the
boxes.

'Not only yours,' Mrs Anson-Pryce reminded her tartly. She
wished the woman would keep silent for a few minutes, but
Hallie Ordway was obviously one of the world's compulsive
talkers. Times of stress always made them worse.

The officers, grim-faced, clustered together. Mrs Anson-
Pryce wondered why Herr von Schreiber was standing next to
Captain Falcon. How had he been allowed into the restricted
area when none of the other passengers had been? Was it
possible that he was the person behind this nightmare?

The sun was dipping towards the horizon. Soon it would be
dark. That would not matter when it came to launching the
lifeboat, but it would make pursuit difficult. If, indeed, pursuit
was planned. It would take time to launch another lifeboat.
Surely, no more lives must be risked.

'Lower away!' The command rang through the air.

Above their heads, davits creaked. No. 1 Lifeboat swung free
of her cradle. Slowly she was wound down to rest parallel with
the Promenade Deck.

Another command was given and two seamen sprang forward to open the gate in the railing, then bent to release the
knots securing the canvas covering over the lifeboat. They
rolled it back and pulled it free, stepping back on to the deck
with it and dropping it at their feet.

There was silence. Even Hallie Ordway had stopped talking,

although her breath came in noisy ragged gasps. Passengers and crew faced each other across the space of open deck, waiting.

The silence lengthened. The rim of the sun touched the horizon. They all seemed caught in a spell from which there was no awakening. To move, to speak, might be to unleash some dark dreaded force. They waited.

Mrs Anson-Pryce became aware of stealthy movement behind her. She turned her head just enough to bring the action into the periphery of her vision. She identified the officer's uniform, the cap pulled low over an unfamiliar face. There were so many junior officers going about business that had no connection with passengers that she never deluded herself that she could recognize them all. But why wasn't this one across the deck with the others?

The quality of Hallie's breathing changed. The breath caught in her throat with a sound between a choke and a moan. She seemed to stumble forward, almost to fall —

Mrs Anson-Pryce felt herself shoved aside as Hallie and the officer pushed past her. They stepped over the rope, moving in unison, and crossed the deck to the open railing.

Now everyone could see clearly the gun held to Hallie's head, forcing her forward. The man cradled a submachine-gun loosely in his other arm.

'Wait a minute —' Mortimer Ordway stepped over the rope farther along the deck and approached the captor and his hostage. 'That's my wife!'

'Is it?' The uniformed man grinned wolfishly. 'Then, if you're interested in keeping her alive, you'd better help me.' He tossed the submachine-gun to Ordway. 'Cover us. If anyone moves, shoot to kill!'

'Oh! Oh God!' Automatically Mortie caught the gun and swung it from crew to passengers and back again unhappily. 'Oh no! Please, please, nobody move! I don't want to have to shoot. But if I have to — to save Hallie — I will!'

No one moved. They believed him.

'Right!' the officer ordered. 'Now load those boxes into the lifeboat! Carefully! Anybody drops one overboard and he's a dead man!'

The crewmen moved forward and picked up the first box. Carefully. They believed him, too.

The officers stared at the bogus figure, half strange, half familiar, trying to identify the stolen uniform. And yet . . . the fit was too perfect . . . the familiarity too close to identification . . .

'Good God!' Captain Falcon choked. 'Good God — *Waring*!'

CHAPTER 18

Waring!

Carl Daniels stood frozen as it all clicked into place. Who had been the first to disappear? The one body no one had seen? *Waring*. When the killer had claimed him as the first victim, no one had doubted it; there had been too many genuine deaths by then.

Who knew the routine of the ship? Who knew which staterooms were unbooked and safe to go to ground in? Who had been in possession of the master key for the safe-deposit boxes and could have had a duplicate made? Who had led shore excursions on previous voyages and could operate No. 1 Lifeboat as a launch? Waring; Waring; Waring, the Assistant Purser.

It explained why deaths among the passengers had so outnumbered deaths among the crew. Either due to lingering friendship, or because of the danger of being recognized if he moved about too freely below decks, Waring had confined most of his depredations to the passengers. Perhaps crew members had been killed only because they had recognized him. That was how he had been able to kill the native crew; accustomed to seeing him about and not knowing that he was assumed to have missed the ship, they had suspected nothing when he had lured them to the lift shaft. It had probably seemed a good joke to them that he had broached the cargo to provide drinks; he was the fourth player in the card game, who had left on the pretext of getting another bottle — and had sent down the lift instead.

It also explained why Joan had been dealt with so lightly when she had caught him returning to the stateroom he had occupied between searches. Waring had always had a soft spot for Joan.

'You know this man?' Otto von Schreiber demanded harshly.

'It's Waring, the Assistant Purser,' Captain Falcon said grimly. 'We thought he was dead. They told us he was the first to go.'

'Some day he will wish that he had been,' von Schreiber vowed.

Hallie stood mute, only an occasional wild roll of her eyes betraying fear and tension. Mortie continued to swing the submachine-gun back and forth, covering everyone on deck.

Waring concentrated on the crewmen piling the boxes into the lifeboat. Aware of this, they moved jerkily, losing their coordination under the cold watching eyes. The last box slipped from their fingers and thudded into the lifeboat.

'Watch it!' Momentarily Waring turned the gun away from Hallie's head, as though to use it on them. Hallie whimpered softly. He restored the gun to its former position immediately. 'Just watch it!' he warned. 'All of you.'

The crewmen backed away, their work finished. They just wanted to keep their heads down and get out of the line of fire.

'I'm taking hostages with me —' Waring divided his message between Captain Falcon and the Purser. 'Just to make sure you don't try anything like dropping the lifeboat too fast, or tilting it. They'll be the first to go overboard — them and the boxes. The passengers wouldn't like that. If you deep-six the boxes here, you'll never get them back.'

'We won't try anything,' Daniels said evenly. 'You have the upper hand, we acknowledge it.' Waring was right. If the boxes went over, they were light enough to be swept for miles by the current before they settled to the bottom where they were small enough to be silted over rapidly. It would be impossible to retrieve them, even if it were possible to find divers foolhardy enough to try. Furthermore, the passengers, having witnessed the irretrievable loss of their fortunes, would for ever after blame the officers who had engineered it, rather than the pirate originally responsible.

'Just keep remembering that.' Waring smiled unpleasantly. 'I'll take these two along with me to make sure that you do. And I'll also take —' His gaze travelled slowly along the assemblage behind the ropes.

They shrank back. Otto von Schreiber tensed as the cold eyes stared at his wife. Cosmo and Connie pressed closer together, heedless of the fact that Pesky was between them; the rift healed, Pesky was inseparable from them once more. In fact, it was only their arms linked through his that held him upright; he was shivering violently and scarcely seemed to be aware of what was happening.

'If you go, I go,' Cosmo whispered.

'Cosmo,—' Connie said softly.

'Me, too.'

'*Her* —' Waring decided.

Heads turned, necks craned. Even the Ordways looked to find their fellow hostage.

'Come on, Joanie,' Waring said. 'Front and centre. You're coming along for the buggy ride. Who knows? You may never want to go back again.'

Joan Fletcher moved forward slowly, as though in a daze. She stooped and slipped under the rope. Her footsteps were unsteady as she approached the lifeboat.

'Wait a minute,' Hallie said. 'What do you want *her* for?'

Mrs Anson-Pryce's eyes narrowed. Hallie Ordway had suddenly stopped behaving like a victim and begun sounding suspiciously like an equal partner.

'Shut up!' Waring cautioned. But it was too late. Some of the others had also begun thinking.

'Cosmo —' Connie whispered. 'She's one of them.'

'They both are!' Mrs Anson-Pryce recognized what had been bothering her for some time: the fact that Hallie had allowed herself to be led away so tamely. The india-rubber double-jointed Hallie, who could have hurled herself sideways and cartwheeled halfway down the deck before her captor could have fired off a shot. She had to be in collusion with this Waring; there had been so many points where she could have escaped. Stepping over the rope — he'd only held a gun loosely at her head; he'd been carrying the submachine-gun in his other hand, unable to restrain her in any way. He'd actually removed the gun from her head when the crewman had dropped the box; she could have ducked out of the line of fire then and her husband could have let off a burst to cut Waring down — if he'd wanted to. The conclusion was inescapable: they were both in it with him.

'You don't need to take any more hostages —' Hallie made an unconvincing stab at acting the martyr. 'You've got us. Don't hurt that poor girl —'

'Shut up,' Waring said again. 'They've rumbled you, you fool. Can't you see that?'

Hallie looked around at the hostile faces — and saw. She was no longer the darling of the mass ratings. Her own face hardened.

Mortimer Ordway brought the submachine-gun to a more businesslike angle. He was no longer holding it unwillingly, almost casually. Their cover was blown. If he killed anyone now, it would not be as a reluctant slayer, forced into it to save his wife; it would be as a deliberate murderer. The Ordways were no longer innocent figures of fun; they were dangerous — and at bay.

'With all they've got —' the shocked question rang out from one of the passengers — 'why are they doing this?'

'All we've got?' Hallie blazed. 'That's all you know! And look at what we had to go through to get it. Week after week on that cruddy quiz show, turning ourselves inside out — making fools of ourselves — so they'd keep us going. Laughing like we thought it was funny when that shit of a Quizmaster called us the Odd-ways and pretended he thought Hallie was short for Halitosis! All I'm sorry about is that he wasn't on board, so we could have killed *him*!'

Truly, we manufacture our own monsters, Mrs Anson-Pryce thought, not without a trace of guilt. She had laughed as heartily as any of the studio audience when the Ordways — such good sports — had been put through their paces like trained seals. No one ever thought to wonder whether the seals enjoyed it. The 'good sports' had learned well — and had been manipulating others, in their turn. She flushed suddenly as she recalled how smoothly they had made her their catspaw for the delegation to the captain. No wonder they had disposed of Edgar so swiftly and malevolently — he had nearly upstaged them.

'Yeah! And all those great prizes!' Hallie jeered. 'Electric mowers, electric carving knives, toothbrushes, microwave ovens, freezers, dishwashers, stereos, air-conditioners, home computers, televisions, humidifiers, video recorders — all that junk. You read the publicity, huh? Wasn't it just great, that bit about, if we switched everything on at once, we could black out a small city? Well, who the hell was going to be able to pay the electricity bill for all of it? Did you ever think of that?'

The answering silence told her that they had not. Most of them had never had to worry about an electricity bill in their lives.

'And those chintzy little diamonds — flawed, at that. Don't think I haven't seen you snobs sneering at them! Oh no, it wasn't as great as they made it sound — not by a long shot. Not until they threw in the *Empress Josephine* and we began to see how we could get a really worthwhile pay-off. Just one big heist and we'd be on Easy Street for the rest of our lives. It was worth the risk.'

'And Waring thought so, too,' Daniels said quietly.

'Sure, why not? He was sick of arse-kissing passengers for lousy tips. We knew there had to be somebody on a ship this size who'd throw in with us — and we needed somebody on the inside. Mortie came down to Florida early to prowl around the bars and sound out the sailors. We struck lucky first go.'

The sun was below the horizon; the moon had not yet appeared. The deck lights came on. Waring moved restively.

'And he had plenty of good ideas of his own. And he could go places we couldn't go —'

'That's enough!' Waring ordered sharply. 'Let's get moving! Into the lifeboat. You first, Joan!'

Joan walked towards the lifeboat unsteadily. No one moved to help her. She looked over her shoulder at the others gathered on the deck; at the *Empress Josephine* itself. Until this voyage, it had been a happy ship, a good berth . . .

'Hurry up!' Waring waved the gun at her — now that he no longer had to keep up the farce of menacing Hallie.

The *Empress Josephine* rolled gently with the swell of the ocean; the lifeboat, several inches away from the edge of the deck, rolled, too. Joan looked down through the gap at the dark sea and the foam of the wash from the prow; she looked away again before she grew too dizzy.

Carl Daniels took an instinctive step forward as she swayed. The submachine-gun swung to point directly at him. Dr Parker laid a restraining hand on his arm.

Daniels drew a deep breath and regained his precarious control. It would do no good at all to let himself be killed making a grandstand play. In his own way, Waring cared for Joan. Joan was clever enough to work on that, once she had got over the shock. The danger was not Waring — but the sudden deep hostility Hallie had displayed. The Ordways were dangerous — possibly mad, by this time — and Joan was a potential witness against them. The longer she was with them, the more she would learn about them — and the worse threat she would become to them. Could Waring protect her if the crunch came?

'Hurry up!'

Joan grasped the railing and stepped down into the lifeboat. The *Empress Josephine* rolled at the last moment and she lost her

footing. She landed heavily on a rumpled blanket at the bottom
of the lifeboat. It was curiously soft and knobbly. On her hands
and knees, she looked up at the deck.

'You next, Hallie —' Waring and Mortimer Ordway were
backing towards the lifeboat, holding their guns on the others.

'Look out below!' Hallie leaped. Her foot landed on a hard
round cylinder and twisted under her. She fell heavily on to the
blanket beside Joan.

Waring stepped down at the other end of the lifeboat to avoid
crowding and overbalancing it. Standing in the prow, he swap-
ped weapons with Ordway and covered the Officers while
Ordway dropped into the lurching lifeboat.

Scanning the deck for possible trouble, Waring gave the
command: 'Lower away!'

'Launch Number One Lifeboat!' the First Mate ordered.

Again davits creaked, the lifeboat swayed and began to sink
below the level of the deck on its slow-motion way to the surface
of the sea.

The passengers broke ranks, ignoring the restraining ropes,
and crossed the deck to the railing. It was as though they wanted
to keep their valuables in sight as long as possible. The ship's
company, too, lined the rail. It might be important to know the
direction the lifeboat had taken when it came to sending out
search planes from the shore. Carl Daniels had eyes only for
Joan, crouched at the bottom of the lifeboat.

Mortimer Ordway had repossessed the submachine-gun and
braced himself against the farther side of the lifeboat, allowing
the muzzle to rise as the lifeboat descended. Daniels hoped the
lifeboat would settle into the water gently; Ordway was so tense
that a jolt might set off a reflex action, spraying the passengers
looking over the rail with bullets.

Waring gave his hand gun to Hallie and made his way to the
tiller, ready to start the engine as soon as they were in the water.
He kicked a fold of the crumpled blanket out of his way,
frowning.

First they had been throwing things at him — and now they were trampling all over him. There was no peace anywhere. Never travel on this ship again!

Dwight Denver Smithers heaved himself to a sitting position, flailing to fight free of the confining blanket. A corner fell away, freeing his head. He was relieved to see the blackness change to a deep navy blue. He continued heaving and hurled himself forward on to hands and knees, colliding with some obstacle as he did so.

It was all right, though, the obstacle went flying out of his way. People seemed to be shouting and cursing all around him. No peace anywhere! Gotta get out of here and find a nice corner in a bar — maybe the sixth bar — and have a nice soothing drink.

The lifeboat swayed perilously. Above, the seamen stopped the machinery lowering it, to give it time to stabilize lest it tilt and send everyone — and everything — into the sea.

'Get him!' Waring shouted into the confusion.

Mortimer Ordway swung the machine-gun towards the heaving mass at the bottom of the lifeboat but held his fire, realizing just in time that a boat riddled with bullets was not going to be particularly seaworthy. He waited for the intruder to stand clear of the hull — when he could cut him down without endangering the lifeboat.

'What are you waiting for?' Hallie shrieked, aiming her own gun. 'Mortie — shoot! Or I will!'

'Wait —' Waring started towards Hallie.

In the momentary confusion, they had forgotten the onlookers at the railing above.

Mrs Anson-Pryce leaned out over the railing, steadied her pearl-handled revolver, then emptied it into the massive target of Mortimer Ordway's body. He dropped the machine-gun and toppled over like a felled tree.

'Mortie!' Hallie screamed. 'Mortie —' Her scream cut off abruptly.

Joan had found the whisky bottle rolling around in the

THE CRUISE OF A DEATHTIME

bottom of the lifeboat. She caught it up and, wielding it like a belaying pin, smashed it over Hallie's head.

D. D. Smithers, having shaken off the blanket, tossed it to one side. It dropped over Waring's head just as D.D. discovered it was almost impossible to stand upright in the lurching lifeboat without support. He threw his arms around the nearest object — bringing Waring down as neatly as if it had been an intentional tackle.

Daniels leaped into the lifeboat and joined the battle. Waring, hampered by both the blanket and D.D.'s boa-constrictor-like grasp, hadn't a chance.

'All right,' Daniels shouted. 'Take us up!'

CHAPTER 19

Mrs Anson-Pryce smiled graciously and tried to ignore the presence beside her. It was all very well — quite touching, really — to be fêted by the President of Nhumbala and one's fellow passengers and to be called a heroine. The lustre was somewhat dimmed, however, by sharing the honours with a hero who was not exactly in the heroic mould.

'Don' mind 'f I do,' D-and-D said as more champagne splashed into his glass. People were getting friendly all of a sudden, now that the voyage was over.

The penthouse restaurant in what passed for a skyscraper in Nhumbala was entirely given over to the passengers and crew of the *Empress Josephine* tonight. From the streets below came the sound of sporadic gunfire, but the revolution was more or less over. The President had assured them that what they heard was simply the 'mopping-up operation'. No one quite liked to dwell on what he might mean by that, but their voyage had sufficiently hardened them to the exigencies of life to enable them to take it in stride.

Some of the passengers were even talking about forming an

Empress Josephine Survivors' Club and holding annual reunions. Mrs Anson-Pryce considered that that was going a little too far. She had no intention of joining. Not that it mattered; the others would probably forget the idea once the euphoria was over. They would soon all be on their separate ways again.

She herself would be heading upcountry in the morning. The President was providing a Guard of Honour to escort her to her property. It was an honour she would be happy to do without; it was unwise to be seen to be too friendly with a dictator. However, she could probably live down the association. Meanwhile, she had reloaded her revolver and had plenty of ammunition.

Some of the others would be returning to Miami on the *Empress Josephine* on the second half of their vaunted cruise. Others would not — and not just the ones who could not.

'I wish you'd change your mind, Mr Smithers —' Pesky leaned across the table and spoke earnestly. He found himself actually getting fond of the old boy, now that he was proved to be innocent. 'Cancel that air ticket and stay on the *Empress Josephine*, the way you originally planned. We're going to have a great trip back.'

'Tell you a li'l secret, ol' boy —' D-and-D waggled a finger at him. 'I may be drunk, but I'm not crazy. Said I'd never travel on that ship again. Nex' time I want a nice quiet voyage I'll take the *Mary Celeste*.'

'I'm sorry, Mr Smithers. I mean, if it was anything I said — Anything I did — Well, I'd like the chance to make it up to you.'

'Ver' kind of you.' D-and-D did not sound grateful. 'Tell you what, you can see me off at the airport 'f you like. Flight leaves at six a.m.'

Cosmo and Connie suppressed giggles. Pesky had thought he was going to sleep late in the morning, without any joggers to pace. It wasn't that funny but, in the sheer bliss of survival, of knowing that they had a future stretching out before them again, they were ready to laugh at anything. Even the trip back wouldn't be so bad, although there'd be uneasy memories around every corner.

Mortimer Ordway was dead. Hallie and Waring were already *en route* back to the States to stand trial. Whether their crimes fell under the jurisdiction of Nhumbala or America was a toss no one was prepared to argue. Whatever they had done, they could not be allowed to languish in a Nhumbalan prison and so they had been smuggled off the ship and on board the first flight to the States. Quite apart from anything else, people would not be willing to return to Nhumbala to act as witnesses at a local trial.

'Your very good health —' Captain Falcon toasted the von Schreibers. They had just toasted him.

'Und success to our plan,' Otto von Schreiber responded. 'I believe we have an excellent case.'

'I'm sure we do,' Captain Falcon said grimly. When the inevitable lawsuits began flying, they were going to launch an offence as the best defence.

Hallie Ordway and Waring were already implicating each other wildly; it would take a Philadelphia lawyer to sort out just who was responsible for each murder. You couldn't believe what people like that said, especially when they were trying to save their own skins.

However, it was fairly certain that Hallie was responsible for the deaths of the elderly couple at the beginning of the voyage. They had been flattered to have a quiz show celebrity knock on their door and enter bearing a bottle of champagne to toast the beginning of the cruise. The girl croupiers, too, had thought nothing of it when Hallie returned to their cabin bearing a tray of sandwiches — Hallie was well-established in the public mind as a sympathetic clown. How could anyone suspect otherwise?

It was too bad that Sparks hadn't been more suspicious. Hallie was a wiry woman with strong hands, she had not found it difficult to strangle him. He had been unconcerned when the ship's minor celebrity wandered into the Radio Room to swap merry quips with him. Until he had abruptly stopped laughing.

Otherwise, Waring had concentrated on the crew, while Mortimer Ordway took care of the passengers. That was Waring's story, but it was quite evident that he had also killed passengers while the Ordways were establishing alibis by making themselves conspicuous. They had roamed everywhere partaking of entertainment — and offering it — making people believe that they were having the time of their lives on the Cruise of a Lifetime.

'We sue the television quiz show,' Otto von Schreiber recapitulated grimly. 'Und we sue the television station — the whole network — because they have placed dangerous lunatics on board our ship. They are responsible for setting the wolves among the sheep. They must pay.'

'We've got a cast-iron case,' Captain Falcon said. 'Anybody would have to be crazy to go on that show in the first place.'

They toasted each other again.

Mrs Anson-Pryce smiled down the table at Joan and Carl, who were also toasting each other. How nice, they seemed to have reached an understanding. They would undoubtedly enjoy the return voyage. If they occasionally thought of some of the missing passengers, they would not dwell unduly on such an unpleasant subject. No one would. The one toast that would never be given was: 'Absent friends'.

'Another toast —' The President, on her other side, jumped to his feet and raised his glass. 'To the hero who cannot be with us tonight: To my Cousin Edgar, who so nobly gave his life in an attempt to save the passengers —'

Well, what else could they have told him? You don't walk up to a notoriously short-tempered and impetuous Dictator and admit that his relative was murdered while locked in the brig after an abortive attempt to take over the ship.

Avoiding each others' eyes, the guests rose and drank the toast to Edgar.

'We will erect a statue to this famous event,' the Dictator assured Mrs Anson-Pryce as they resumed their seats. 'To the gallant *Empress Josephine* and the noble Edgar. I visualize something in black marble by the crocodile pool . . .'

'How very fitting,' Mrs Anson-Pryce murmured.